# UNFORESEEN PARTITIONS II

## Keeta B.

Unforeseen Partitions II by Keeta B.

Cover design by BlackEncryption Designs

Book design and format by SteamyTPub

Printed in the United States of America

Steamy Trails Publishing:
www.steamytrailspublishing.com

ISBN-10:0-9988994-0-2
ISBN-13:978-0-9988994-0-4

# *DEDICATION*

This book is dedicated to my readers, supporters and to the believers or my passion.

# Table of Contents

# *INTRODUCTION*

*Unforeseen Partitions II* continues every bit of the passion and lust from the erotic short stories in part I. Creatively written by Keeta B. and guest writers author Keybae and Matthew Shephard, the winners of the 2016 Unforeseen Partition II contest.

This book is intended to open your mind to love and lust, while tantalizing your inner soul with passion. If you thought the first edition was a hot read, wait until you open this one and begin reading. Cuddle up with a glass of your favorite intoxicating drink, a warm blanket, and candlelight, or with your lover, allowing this book to take you on an erotic ride.□

## INTRODUCING MATTHEW SHEPHARD

Matthew Shephard was born and raised in Fort Worth, Texas. He is a graduate of the University of Texas at Arlington, where he earned his bachelor's in Sociology. He has been writing and performing poetry locally since 2011, starting with a piece written for the love of his life and won our 2015 poetry contest, which earned him a full page featuring is unique poetry.

Matthew has authored three short collections of poetry entitled, "love headaches & heartbreaks", "speak life", and "the art of starvation". He is currently working on a fourth collection. He credits God and both of his loving parents, Tammie & Willie Shephard, for his hard work ethic and talent.

# ELEMENTARY SCHOOL

Two plus two equals four,

And…

Four comes before play,

Meaning…

Foreplay is the math game you play in class right before you eat lunch.

Then you go to recess where the unapologetic motto of "Go hard or take yo soft *ss home!" was born.

So, I start by kissing and caressing every curve and crevice on your body like I'm worshipping a goddess.

Subtract all your clothes and add them to the list of things you will never need to worry about while with me.

Now let's multiply the intensity.

Enjoy the spine-tingling sensation of me dividing your legs in two.

Now scream,

Like the bell that signifies the end of class and the beginning of lunch….

Perfect gentleman,

Manners minded,

Sticky face, clean plate, hands bound behind your back.

Don't push me away,

Let me stay inside and allow my taste buds to become best buds with the taste of your love.

Feed me until the belly of the savage beast within aches in fullness.

Now release….and let it rain.

We always had more fun at recess after it rained….

Full speed ahead we'd run out of the building and onto the playground.

First, I lift you up and let you hang from the monkey bars,

Swing back and forth as long as your heart desires.

Kick towards ecstasy and push away from the constraints applied under the pressure of adulthood.

Slide down just enough to put your head in the clouds every time you bounce up and down on the seesaw.

Hop on the merry go round and allow me to spin you so fast that not even the hands of gravity himself could slow you down.

So you just have to JUMP………OFF!

Which you always manage to do just in time.

When the whistle blows to send us back in for naptime,

I watch you sleep wondering if I should be gone,

But then you grab me and tell me, "I went hard so I ain't gotta take my soft *ss home!"

Written by 2015's Poetry Contest Winner, Matthew Shephard.

# BOY NEXT DOOR

"Ah, the fresh air, cool breeze, and this ice-cold margarita is hitting the spot," I exclaimed.

It was late summer, and I was sitting in my favorite reclining lounge chair on my screened-in back patio watching the sun go down. The temperature was still blazing well over the hundred-degree marker and the sun was finally going down. The smell of barbeque was in the air and I was getting awfully hungry.

"Let me be nosey and see if my fine, sexy ass neighbor is cooking up something delicious today. I sure could use a plate," I said.

Rico was this light-skinned, chiseled, six pack sporting, low hair-cut, tatted up, six-foot tall, Jordan wearing brotha who could grill his ass off. However, Rico was living with another woman. Rico and his live-in, Renee', had been my neighbors for approximately three to four years now. I first laid eyes on him one day when I came outside in my nightgown to check the mailbox. Like all the times before, never paying much attention to what's going on around me, I wandered out to the mailbox with my duster on, rollers and all. Then I heard this deep voice call out from next door. "Well, good morning. How are you doing, ma'am? My name's Rico. I'm your new neighbor." Instantly my mouth dropped. *Who in the hell was that fine ass specimen?* was the first question to come to my mind.

Dropping the mail up the driveway, I hauled ass into the house. Once inside, I put my back against the door, yanked out all the rollers, wiped the sweat from my forehead, and said a prayer that this fine ass Al B. Sure looking brotha didn't come knocking at my door. Moments later, my damn doorbell rings. *Who the hell could it be?* Looking out the peep hole, I saw a cute little five-foot-five inch, brown-skinned girl with short, natural brown, curly hair. She had an oval face, wide eyes, and a slim waist, and since this is my first time seeing her, maybe she's some kin to the guy next door. Opening the door, I said, "Hello, may I help you?"

"Hello, ma'am. I brought you your mail you dropped. My boyfriend said you were in a hurry so I decided to bring it to you and come say hello," the young girl replied.

"Why thank you. It's very nice of you. My name's Rita, and you are?"

"My name's Renee' and it's a pleasure meeting you."

Wondering how old this young couple was really started to puzzle my brain. I'm a young, vibrant thirty-five years old, but these two can't be any more than twenty-six to twenty-nine. Just babies, but I'm glad to see they got their heads on straight by getting them a decent place to stay. That shows stability in my book.

I'm tall for a female, standing at five-foot-nine inches, with a cute, heart shaped face. Dimples encompass each cheek like targets, and I wear my hair in a short, boy style cut, almost reminding me of one worn by Meagan Good. I look damn good for my age, to say the least. Most people wouldn't believe me if I told them I was thirty-five. That's why it pleases me when I see young people doing well for themselves like the couple next door.

After the new couple finished moving all of their items into their new place, I noticed smoke coming from the backyard. While I was sitting on my patio I heard someone knocking at my front door. I went into the house to see who it could possibly be. It was Renee' again.

"Hello, I don't mean to bother you again, but my boyfriend told me to come over and ask you if you would like to come over and have some barbeque and drinks with us. He's a really cool guy and good when it comes to grilling and shit talking. I think you would enjoy yourself."

"Well, let me think about it, Renee'. I was just enjoying some peace and quiet in my own back yard. Maybe a little later," I responded.

An hour and a half or so had passed by since Renee' had left my place. I must have dozed off. The smoke had filled my back yard and it smelled totally delicious. Made me very curious to see what Mr. Rico had cooked up over there. If he was that good on the grill no telling what he was like in bed. Oh my, I need to get my mind right before something happens we both will regret. However, since I was invited over for barbeque, barbeque is what I'm going to get.

I got up from my chair, went into the house, found a nice revealing outfit to put on with a matching pair of sandals, and then I fixed my hair. As I finished getting dressed I sprayed on my J. Lo perfume and walked out the door. There were other guests arriving as I was making my way over. They had the side fence unlocked as the point of entrance. As I entered, Rico and I made eye contact. He noticed I looked a million times different than when he saw me at the mailbox earlier that day. Even though he was casually dressed in basketball shorts and a wife beater, it was something about him that enticed my curiosity. He was really doing it up big. He had smoked links, red hot links, ribs, hot dogs, hamburgers, chicken, pork steaks, potatoes, and corn on the cob. Renee' had made potato salad, deviled eggs, baked beans, and a few cakes and pies for desert. Rico's buddies had brought any and every kind of beer you could possibly think of to drink. There was a liquor bar and Jell-O shots. These young people have moved in and know how to kick it. They are doing it up big time.

While fixing my plate, Rico came up to me and asked if I was enjoying myself.

"Of course, I am. I am a party of one. I thought you knew that?"

The music was banging, making it very difficult to hear, but it seemed as if everyone around was having just as good of a time as I was.

Rico lened into my ear and uttered, "Just wanted to make sure, Ma. Didn't want to be a host and not make sure my guests were having a good time, especially when they looking and smelling as good as you. You almost make me want to taste every drop of what you have to offer."

"I'm truly flattered by your kindness and blunt suggestions, Rico, but I won't disrespect your girl or your house like this by engaging in this type of conversation with you. Thank you so much for the invite. I think this is my que to go now. You have a great day."

Grabbing my plate, I left and headed home. Knowing good and damn well I wanted to stay so I could observe Rico's fine ass some more. But, I didn't want to come off disrespectful to his lady, Renee'. It's not cool to come to someone else's home knowing they have a man and try and push up on them in front of the significant other. I'd never want anyone to do it to me so I sure as hell was not about to do it to anyone else. However, I would fuck the hell out of Rico and not give a damn about little Miss Renee'. That's a totally different story. While watching, Rico work his magic on the grill, the way he was flipping those meats gave me the perfect opportunity to get a good look at his meat through those basketball shorts he had on. That dick of his had a print as big as my foot. Any woman would have had her eyes glued to his crotch just like I did. Oh well, instead of wondering about coulda, shoulda, woulda, next door, I decided to pour me a glass of wine, sit on my back patio with my headphones on listening to my Mp3 player, and stare at the moon high in the sky.

As I gazed into the night sky, it took me to a fantasy place. All the men and women any person could dream of were at their fingertips. Romance was in the night air, lovemaking music could be heard in the background. Sexual healing was going down. Every man and woman around was having sex with each other filled with passion and desire. You could feel the fire from their skin and see the passion in their eyes. The intensity with which they thrusted their bodies against one another was sexual gratification. This dream was more than a swinger's party delight. This was a down right orgy with all the works and perks of sexual exploration for any person's personal desire. Self-consciously, I could feel my panties getting wet just from the thought of the sexual gratification from the erotic tranquility that electrifies my inner being. Just as I'm lusting in the glorification of this moment, I'm awakened by a knock at the door.

I wasn't expecting any company. My only plans were to enjoy the rest of the food from Rico's, this glass of wine, and the great outdoors before calling it a night. I stormed to the door.

"Who is it?" I said.

"It's me, Rico," replied the voice on the other side of the door.

Curious to see what brought him over I opened the door.

"What is it, Rico? I don't have time for no bullshit ass games!"

"I'm sorry, Mami. Please accept my apology. I didn't mean to disrespect you in any way. Creo que eres la mujer más Beautifulest que he visto . Me gustaría llegar a conocerte mejor. You are the most beautifulness woman I've seen. I would like to get to know you better. This is real shit, ma, believe that."

"Acepto que disculpa todo yo tiempo que sabes que no me rompo hogares felices. Usted y su novia parece feliz y que planea dejarlo así como así. I accept your apology as long as you know I will not break your happy home. You and your girlfriend seem happy and I plan to leave it just like that. Yeah, you didn't think I would respond back now, did ya?"

"Well, Rita let's get some things perfectly straight. I'm an honest guy and I have no reason to lie to you. I like what I see, and what I see is you. Renee' and I have been kicking it for over six years now, but she knows I don't do or like relationships. But she insists on telling people that I'm her boyfriend and that we are together. I've told her over and over again about that shit but she continually does it when I'm not around, thinking it's not going to get back to me. She's a good girl and all, but she knows how I like my space and I like to do the things that single people do. What Renee' and I have is considered an understanding and sometimes it gets a little distorted on her end. You know you females are emotional creatures and when they smell another woman invading what they consider their territory, they get jealous and overprotective. She sniffed you from the time we pulled the truck up in the yard so I already knew you must be one fine piece of work."

"So, you mean to tell me you still sent Renee' over here to invite me to your little shin dig knowing she felt some type of way about me just to get a rise out of her? What type of shit is that? Who on earth would go out of their way to do some mess like that? That was cruel, unnecessary, down-right mean, and disrespectful. You didn't take her feelings into consideration or mine. How the hell you going to come over here with this bullshit thinking I'm supposed to believe anything you have to say and you have disrespected the woman you live with already? Get the fuck outta here and don't come back until you learn some manners and self-respect for others."

Rico didn't like the way I came off to him. He grabbed me up by my arms, planted his mouth over mine, and began to kiss me and caress me in places my body had been yearning for quite some time. The feeling of euphoria came over me. My temperature was heightened and juices began to flow. If I wasn't ready for any action before, I was certainly ready at this given moment. I began trying to fight Rico and say no, but my body was giving him all the signs of saying yes. How could I deny this fine ass man? He lay me down on the floor in the living room and climbed on top of me.

From the weight of his body I could feel the fully erect, hardness of his dick on my thigh. At that moment, every fantasy a person could have ever dreamed about was about to become a reality right there in my living room. Rico took both of my legs and spread them above my head. He pulled my pants and panties off with one hand, exposing my clean shaven pussy. With the other hand he opened up my pussy exposing my clit and inside walls. He started teasing me with his fingers, making me wetter and wetter. Once he noticed my juices were beginning to flow, he started sucking and licking on my clit, sending me into spastic convulsions.

After getting a mouth full of my wetness, Rico pulled down his shorts exposing his fully erect dick. He looked at me and said, "How you want this dick? Covered or raw? It's however you want it. Really it's up to you." After the way, he just ate my pussy, I wanted to take every inch of that dick in me without anything between us. Normally, I wouldn't take suck a risk on the first go around, but as horny as this man just made me feel this was a risk I'm willing to take.

Rico started flipping me every which way possible. He went into my kitchen and grabbed a bowl of fresh fruit, whipped cream, and other items. The music from my Mp3 player was still playing. R. Kelly was sending out instructions for his, "12 Play" groove. Our bodies were in sync, moving to the rhythm of the music. Keith Sweat was soon to follow on the playlist of music. The way I was sucking Rico's dick had me wanting to do more and more things with this man. I decided to grab my Crown Royal bag I had hidden from behind the couch that contained my Pop Rocks, small container of Listerine, Cinnamon discs, anal Eze, jar of whipped cake frosting, a zip locked bag containing three large grapefruits, and Halls brand cough drops. Rico's toes curled from the way I would tease the head of his dick with my tongue. I took in the entire length of his dick, deep throated it, spit on it, and suck the juices up with my mouth. While sucking his dick, I began using both hands to help stroke, and then just one. Once I was comfortable enough with my performance I didn't use any hands at all, only my mouth to please the man I was enjoying sexually at the moment. The slurping noise alone sent invigorating sexually arousing sensations into both our bodies. The juices from my pussy plus the music were like a Beethoven's Symphony precisely played. Each instrument struck their notes accordingly. It was a remarkable event.

Rico looked at me and said, "You're nothing but an ol' freak!" We both busted out in laughter. The breeze from the patio door made the moment even better. Oh shit, the patio door!

"Rico, get up! Get up!" I screamed. "Did I forget to close the gotdamn patio door?"

"Chill, Ma," Rico vocalized. "It's just a damn sliding door. Who gives a damn? We over here having a good ass time and you worried about a fucking door. Who the hell does that type of shit? Ma, you really need to stop bugging out. Now come over here and get some more of this dick before I have to get back to my party next door. I'm trying to give you some special attention but you fucking up my mood real quick with this bullshit."

"I guess you're right, Rico. Could have sworn I saw someone standing at the door while we were getting it in. Maybe I was wrong but like you said who cares. It could be nothing and I'm over here tripping. Let me enjoy the moment while we have it. So let me ride this kangaroo stick you got, Papi, and show you who's in control."

Rico and I sexed for what seemed like hours. The sun had gone down and the smoke from his grill was just barely visible. We both took a shower and freshened up. I asked Rico wouldn't it seem odd him going back home smelling like Ivory soap when he should have the aroma of barbeque? He looked at me and replied, "Are you worried about what Renee' has to say, because I'm not. Fuck her." He gave me a kiss on the lips and told me he would hit me up later.

Closing the door behind him, I let out a sigh. Wow, what the hell just happened? I couldn't have seen this coming to save my life. Not regretting it did by any means, but didn't think it would happen this soon. I decided to clean up our mess so I could get a good night's rest. I had things to do the next day.

The next morning, while getting in my car, I noticed Renee' in the yard. Being polite, I waved and spoke like the previous day. I noticed she had a smug look on her face and had a vague attitude about her. I brushed it off.

"Wonder what's got her panties all in a knot this morning. Rico and Renee' must have had a falling out about something. Oh well, not my issue, not my beef so no need for me to worry my pretty little head about it."

So, I went about my daily routine for the day. When I arrived back home, I noticed Rico was outside in the yard. He was standing in the driveway looking over some car parts, getting prepared to work on his 1972 Chevelle SS. That baby was a bad ass. When him and Renee' first moved in, I remembered seeing this beauty loaded up on the trailer and I thought how she would light the fire under someone's ass someday with the right love and care. He must have noticed me when I got out of my car. He gave a little wink as I walked by, then continued what he was doing as if nothing happened. I giggled and walked into the house.

Entering the house, I thought to myself what woman on this earth could live with a man under the type of conditions that Renee' did and allow him to treat her in such a manner? He blatantly disrespects her but she loves him just the same. Does she not know he couldn't care less about her, her feelings, or anything else she has to offer for that matter? He's only using her ass for a place to lay, stay, and do what the fuck he wants to, but she obviously doesn't see the shit. I don't want to call her dumb, but she sure seems to fall into the dumb category. Maybe she is just blinded by love. If that's the case, can't fault her too much, I've been there once or twice in this life time. It can fuck a person's mindset up, so I know how she feels.

Rico and I started to spend more time together. He began coming over more and more at night and we would drink and have sex. We soon progressed to the point of getting to know one another on a more personal level. During one of our many conversations, I found out Rico was 27 years old, of Black and Puerto Rican descent, has four brothers and six sisters, was once prescribed Xanax due to a tragic incident that occurred during childhood, and never in life had a serious relationship. Other than the minor things, he really was a cool guy. The macho man persona he put on was for his homies and he could've really chilled because he wasn't fooling anyone with it. Rico was truly a kind, loving, and considerate person who wants, needs, and desires love and compassion just like any and everyone else in life. He pretended he didn't so no one saw the softer side of him and thought of him as weak.

After a few months or so had passed of him coming over, Rico decided he didn't care what time of day it was he showed up or who saw him. He didn't try to hide the fact that he was over here or lie when he was going back home. If, during his visits, we had hot passionate day or night sex and passion marks were left, he wore them proudly. He never attempted to hide them or deny where they came from.

The more time Rico and I spent together, the dirtier the looks I began getting from Renee'. One day, she decided she was going to confront me in my own front yard.

"How could you? I trusted you and you went behind my back and fucked my man? You old ass bitch. You no different than the rest of them hoes he fucked with. Just like he ran through they ass, he gonna do you the same way," Renee' shrieked.

This bitch then had the audacity to spit on me. Can you believe that? Before I knew it, I had clocked the hell outta that stupid ass broad. I had her ass laying out on the ground like I was Sugar Ray Leonard. The most disrespectful thing you can do to someone is spit on them. Un-huh, I don't play that shit; she really had me fucked all the way up.

Now all of a sudden, she worried about who her so-called man was fucking. The bitch should have been worried about who he was fucking way before me. Now she mad. I'm about to give her something way more to be mad about too. See, I'm no dummy. I knew Rico's slick ass wasn't just fucking me. It'd been four years now and he didn't spend nearly as much time over here as he used to. He'd always gone somewhere with somebody, but I wasn't the one complaining. Let his ass do what he fucking does.

A real woman knows! It doesn't take a rocket scientist to know when he go home and she boo-hooing, and shit he feels sorry for her ass, curses her out, then gives in to that bullshit and fucks her too!

That's okay though, from now on there is going to be some pettiness in the air. I'm going to let her ass know each and every time he kiss her it's my pussy she tastes all up in her mouth. Every time she sucks his dick it's my pussy juices that cover his dick. Every time she thinks she trying something new with his punk ass it's because we already tried the shit. Bitches need to learn they roles and play they positions, but she will learn by the time I get finished. Bet she won't come with this bullshit to another female ever in life. She thought she was one crazy ass female by trying to confront me. She has finally met her match.

When Rico pulled up, he heard the commotion and saw what happened. He got out of his car and ran over to my place where we both were still in the yard. He picked me up and asked if I was okay. From my facial expression, the reassurance was undeniable. We could hear Renee' cursing and swearing but nobody gave a damn. Rico and I walked into the house, put on my music from my Mp3, and allowed the flow of it to take us to that musical escapade only it could take us too. From the sultry souls of Luther, Johnny, Kelly, and The Isley Brothers, just to name a few. We could hear Renee' banging and pounding on my door. She must have done this until her hands got tired. Since she decided to come to me with this bullshit by banging on my door and what not, I made sure I fucked her so-called man until my legs, mouth, body, and head got tired so I guess we were even. We both were tired.

It's a dangerous game getting involved with the boy next door. It was never my intention to sleep with him, let alone have it go on for the amount of time it did. Rico was good eye candy. There was nothing wrong with two people flirting with one another and making eye contact every now and again. During this entire ordeal I found that I had caught some feelings for this man, but I never allowed them to let me lose sight of bigger fish in the pond. Rico had some good dick, but dick comes a dime a dozen, and I have plenty of dimes. My bank account stays fat.

Guess the saying is true, "Everything that glitters ain't gold." All this mess I went through with Renee' and Rico wasn't even called for. Letting my ego and pride get the best of me and allowing his sexual drive to entice me to do things I shouldn't have done under those circumstances. Lesson learned.

# CHECK MATE

I should have known better

Just when I thought love didn't live here anymore

You entered my heart as if it was a revolving door

You made me feel like the woman I became back in '94

Now here I am rolling my Dutch, yearning for your touch

Looking at my phone praying that you hit my line

Wondering if I've even crossed your mind

How did we go from sucking and fucking to dodging and ducking?

From intimate nights to not a soul in sight?

Can't you see I'm falling apart?

Baby, please stop taunting my heart

You have people thinking I'm sick

But in all actuality, I just need your dick

I wanna hear your laugh

And feel my muscles contract as I move up and down your shaft

I wanna feel you in my inner soul

Then swallow that thang whole

I wanna make love in the rain

Until we both are physically and mentally drained

I wanna hear you say, "Damn, that's all me" and "Don't stop, Key."

But now you're gone and I am alone

Reliving all this pain while feeling shame

I should've known from the start that you would tear me apart and suck all the blood from my heart

I should've known that you would eventually leave

I should've known that love ain't shit but make believe

# *PLAYING WITH FIRE*

<u>Turk Rollins</u>

Buzz. Buzz. Buzz.
"Cell block 27," Officer J. Anderson replied as he answered the buzz.
The person on the intercom answered, "Send Inmate Rollins, Turk, number 11986 down for a visit."

Officer Anderson replied, "Sure thing, I'll send him down, Shorty."

The guard yelled into dayroom area of Cell block 27. "Inmate Rollins, Turk, number 11986, you have a visitor. Grab your ID card and come up front."

"Wonder who the hell here. I ain't expecting any visitors, especially at this hour," I replied. "I'm not expecting anyone until tomorrow around eleven in the morning when my ol' lady shows up for our normal visit. Whoever this is, it better be worth my time. Shit, interrupting our Spades game."

By the way, my name is Turk Edward Rollins III. I'm 35 years young and was born on May 22, 1980. Originally from Austin, Texas, but living in Atlanta before I caught my case. I'm currently housed at the Huntsville Correctional Facility on an attempt to manufacture and deliver drugs greater than four grams. The judge sentenced me ten to twenty years and I've been down eight. I should have been eligible for early release several times but the bitch ass parole officer obviously hasn't been doing their fucking jobs. I'm in on a non-violent charge with no prior history of arrests. There is no way in hell I should have sat doing this much time. Now, all of a sudden, I have a mysterious visitor coming to see me at eight o'clock at night. This had better be good or somebody is going to catch hell.

I put my ID card in the front pocket of my prison uniform, then proceeded to the front of the dorm style dayroom, passing my ID card through the slot for the guards to scan. I'm then instructed to wait for the buzzer and pass through the open door so one of the two officers on the opposite side could pat search me. Once the pat search was complete, Officer Cromwell escorted me down the corridor to the visitation area. Inside the large cafeteria style room, the officer instructs me to have a seat at the middle table with both my hands face down on it until my visitor arrived. I complied with the directions given to me. While sitting in the room, I noticed I was the only one in the visitation area and the room was quiet and still. I was puzzled. There was still approximately forty-five minutes of visiting hours remaining.

After a few minutes passed, in walked this dark mocha chocolate, long flowing hair, doe eyed honey wearing a business suit and stilettos, carrying a briefcase in one hand with a stack of papers in the other. I've never seen this beauty before. She must be somebody new. I found myself gazing at her as she approached the table where I was sitting. She then walked over, placed the papers and briefcase on the table, and extended her hand for me to shake.

"Good evening, Mr. Rollins. I apologize for disturbing you at this hour. My name is Deputy O'Conner, and I am the new in-house parole officer."

"Good evening, Miss, Ms., or is it Mrs. O'Conner? How is it I have the pleasure of meeting you?"

"For starters, Mr. Rollins, it's Ms. O'Conner, and as I stated, I am the new in-house parole officer. The last one, Mr. James, had a situation he needed to tend to that required someone to fill in his position. In his absence, he left plenty of paperwork that had not been addressed and this is where I come in. Now with all that being said, Mr. Rollins, let's begin. For verification purposes I need for you to state your full government name, date of birth, current age, and give your identification number."

With my head racing eighty miles an hour, I missed every word this woman spoke. Damn little mama sexy as hell. The more I found myself looking at her, the more I noticed. She has these long, slender legs, tight ass calf muscles, firm juicy lips, tight hips, and a set of firm tits. Shit had my dick throbbing sitting here looking at her.

"Um, excuse me. Mr. Rollins, did you hear what I just said?" Ms. O'Conner asked.

I quickly snap back and replied, "Yes, Ms. O'Conner. I apologize. I was thinking about what brought you hear to speak with me in such urgency."

Ms. O'Conner looked me in the eyes and said, "We can discuss all of that. First, I need for you to answer the questions at hand. Now can we begin? Name, date of birth, current age, and identification number, please."

I slowly began. "My name is Turk Edward Rollins III. I was born on May 22, 1980. I am currently thirty-five years old and my identification number is 11986."

"Thank you, Mr. Rollins," Ms. O'Conner replied. "Next question: Do you have any identifying marks, scars, tattoos, burns on your body not previously notated or disclosed?"

"No ma'am, I don't, Ms. O'Conner," I said.

"Have you received any disciplinary actions in the last ninety days? If so, please disclose the reason and length of time."

Fuck, this bitch starting to get on my nerves. I could lie to the hoe, but that wouldn't solve shit. I know good and gotdamn well she had all the paperwork in front of her but she wanted to ask these dumb ass questions.

"Yes, Ms. O'Conner I have. I spent thirty days in the hole for assault on another inmate."

"By any chance, Mr. Rollins, do you have any gang affiliation or feel you have aggressive behavior?"

"No, Ms. O'Conner. I do not have any gang affiliation, nor do I feel I have aggressive behavior. I assaulted the guy but only after he attacked me."

"I see in the disposition that you wrote, you stated you were physically attacked while in the shower and that you only defended yourself. Is this a true attest of your statement, Mr. Rollins?" Ms. O'Conner inquired.

"Yes, ma'am, those are indeed the facts."

I was sitting there wondering where in the hell was this woman going with all these damn irrelevant questions. This bitch bet not be here on some mess or trying to pin something else on me. I'll snap on this hoe quicker than a pregnant woman can snap back after giving birth.

I stared at Ms. O'Conner as if she was a target. She wrote down a few things on her note pad, then looked up. "Well, Mr. Rollins as I stated when I first arrived, I'm here to finish up the paperwork Mr. James left upon his untimely departure. All the questions I ask of you are for your benefit. I am here to tell you that you were eligible for parole three months ago and for whatever reason Mr. James did not complete your packet. However, I'm here to assure you that if he had, your incarceration would not have taken place, because you would have been a free man. By the end of the week, I will have processed all your paperwork and submitted it to the releasing department. They will contact you to make out your parole plan and ensure you have transportation when you are released. How does that sound, Mr. Rollins?"

"Shit sounds damn skippy if you ask me, Ms. O'Conner. I really appreciate you taking the time out of your schedule to come see me. I apologize if I came off a little rude in the beginning. I'll just be glad when all of this is over," I said.

"Mr. Rollins, you know where my office is located. If you need to contact me in regards to your release, fill out a request form and drop it in the box, or stop by and I'll be glad to answer whatever questions you may have."

"Oh, I'm sure you will see me again, Ms. O'Conner. You have a good night."

We both stood, and once again, she extended her hand for me to shake. This time I held onto her hand a little longer than I should have. She snatched it away, picked up her papers from the table and left. I hoped she felt the vibe I was giving off. If not, I would have to work that much harder. I'm making it my business to see her fine ass as much as possible before I jump ship. She damn near had my dick rock hard by just staring at her ass. Took everything I had in me to contain myself. This Black beauty had captured my attention and I needed to act upon it.

Later that evening, I found myself daydreaming about fucking the hell outta Ms. O'Conner. I had envisioned that tight ass bent over her desk with her skirt hiked up, panties pulled to the side, and this eight-inch dick plowing all up in that ass. I could feel the wetness from the juices flowing from her pussy. Yeah, I need some of that in my life. Now I just have to find the right reasons to pay her a visit.

The next morning, I had devised a plan. I put in my request to see Ms. O'Conner. All I needed to do was wait for them to call the pod and request for me to come down to her office. The wait was making me anxious as hell, but I knew it would be well worth it. I didn't know if I was more anxious about seeing Ms. O'Conner again or the fact that I was going home soon. What I did know was ever since I'd been back in my pod, I couldn't stop thinking about her fine ass. Each time my mind wandered, it focused on her and caused my dick to thump like a rabbit in my pants. This shit had to end, but not before I got a piece of Ms. O'Conner's pussy.

At approximately 10:45 in the morning, the intercom in the officer's booth buzzed. I'm praying they're calling for me. I needed to see Ms. O'Conner before they gave recreation call. I had some business to handle on the rec yard that afternoon. Get it together, Rollins. She's just another woman, I thought to myself. But, the reality of it all was she's not just another woman. She's the woman I needed to fulfill this urge I was feeling. She's the prettiest thing this side of the fence I've seen in a mighty long time. Don't get me wrong. My lady from the outside was no small change when it came to looks. My baby banging from head to toe, but right now she couldn't feed this appetite of mine. I needed this fine ass chocolate drop that had my mind turning flips. Ms. O'Conner.

I didn't know what it was about Ms. O'Conner that had me feeling this way. Could be the fact she's off limits and I'm not supposed to have her, or it could just be a mere attraction that would soon fade away. Whichever it is, only time would tell.

Once again, my thoughts were interrupted by the guard calling my name. "Rollins you're wanted in the front office. Grab your ID card and come to the front," the guard yelled.

I knew what time it was, so I quickly gathered my items and headed to the front of the housing unit. The same procedures, whether you are entering or exiting, applied when it comes to the housing unit. ID cards were passed through the port and scanned by the guard, then the inmate was thoroughly pat searched. The guard finished his pat search and instructed me to wait for the buzzer and open the door. Another guard was on the opposite side waiting to escort me down the corridor.

As I approached Ms. O'Conner's office, I was instructed to stand next to the wall, and when she was ready for me she would come out and get me. I did as I was told and waited for her door to open. Several minutes passed and her door finally opened. Another inmate walked out, nodded his head, and winked. She then acknowledged for me to enter her office. She closed the door behind her and motioned for me to pick a chair on the opposite side of the desk to have a seat. I chose the chair closest to the door. Just in case something strange went down, I could make a run for it. I sat down and started observing everything about Ms. O'Conner. The sway in her hips, the color of her eyes, and the formation of her lips had my dick swollen. I watched as she picked up a manila folder with my name and ID number on it. She looked me in the eyes like she did the first night and spoke, "Mr. Rollins, I received a request form from you to see me. Is there something I could help you with?"

I had already rehearsed my lines so I knew exactly how to respond, so I told her I came to get more information on my release. "How do I go about submitting this paperwork to have someone come and pick me up versus using public means of transportation? Also, to whom do I send the paperwork to for my sponsor for my parole plan? And, exactly what did the parole board look at to determine my eligibility for parole? You mentioned I was supposed to be released months ago. Do you think you could investigate more and see if it could have been longer?" I asked.

Ms. O'Conner reached down to her file drawer, started flipping through some papers, and pulled one out. She then leaned across the desk and handed me the sheet of paper. "This should answer those common questions you were concerned about, Mr. Rollins. Is there anything else I could assist you with?" Ms. O'Conner replied.

Sitting in the chair watching her as she wrote down some notes, I begun thinking that I wasn't quite ready to leave her office yet so I had to think fast. I knew the next few words out of my mouth would be totally out of line but what the hell, it's worth a shot. "Um, yes, Ms. O'Conner, I do have something I would like to ask you. Why would a fine ass woman like yourself choose this type of environment to work in? I mean you sexy as hell. Why would you want to work amongst all male hardened criminals in this type of setting? Many of these men haven't seen a woman in many a moons, making you a target for something bad to happen."

With a raised eyebrow, Ms. O'Conner shifted in her seat to cross her legs, clear her throat, and responded. "For your information, Mr. Rollins, I am totally capable of handling myself. According to the degree I hold, my experience and knowledge of my position makes me very capable of working in any type of environment, even if it's one like this."

Mumbling under my breath, I replied, "Hell, if I didn't think you couldn't handle yourself, one thing you wouldn't have to be bothered with is me putting myself out there to protect you."

"Excuse me? Mr. Rollins did you say something?" Ms. O'Conner asked.

"Um, no ma'am that's all. You have a good day," I said.

Walking back to my pod, my dick was hanging down my leg. I had to shield myself with the papers Ms. O'Conner had given me so no one would notice. I have got to get a piece of that ass from Ms. O'Conner. Shit, she makes a brother want to do something real nasty with her. Fuck, I couldn't shake this lady from my thoughts.

I knew my girl, Meeka, knew something was up during visitation. She gave me some head over by the soda machine and the way I was plowing my dick down her throat it was obvious my mind was somewhere else. Yeah, it was. I was envisioning it was Ms. O and nobody else. The more and more I thought about it, I saw her face and all I could think about was fucking the life out of her.

Finally arriving back to my bunk, my train of thought was rudely interrupted by this cat I knew from the outside world named T-Rock. "Hey, Ro. You think you can spare a soup? My gal hasn't had time to put no money on my books and I'm hungry as hell. I promise to pay you back soon as my money hit," T-Rock said.

"Sure, man. One soup ain't gone break me, but you make sure you pay me back. I've heard about you and your shenanigans," I responded.

T-Rock shook his head, promising to repay the debt, so I gave him the soup and sent him on his way. I lay back on my bunk to take a quick nap. It would be rec time soon and I needed to head to the yard.

"Yard call! Yard call! If any of you are going to the yard this is the time to do so!" the guard working the door yelled.

Quickly, I jumped up, threw some water on my face, and headed out the door.

While on the yard, I made some transactions and settled some disputes with some folks I considered to be like a brother. One of my folks approached and asked to have a few words with me, saying it was imperative and of great importance. We decided to walk the track so it wouldn't be as obvious that he was giving me information and look more like we were exercising.

My informant told me to watch my back when it came to T-Rock and especially my girl, Meeka. He got word that they were trying to set me up on some hoe ass shit that could be detrimental to my life and well-being. I told him to give me some details about dates, times, and whatever else he had. He began telling me how he witnessed Meeka during one of our visits stick around afterward and sit at the table with T-Rock. My informant said he witnessed Meeka pass a small cellphone to him, and upon leaving, she bent over and kissed him. On another occasion, he overheard T-Rock on the phone speaking to a lady, discussing business and how he was going to take over and the person wouldn't even see it coming.

We finished our walk and gave each other some dap. I told him to expect a package from an anonymous individual soon for his loyalty and information.

I wondered how T-Rock's time had gotten reduced when he'd never put in an appeal or gone to court. Something had smelled fishy for quite some time. Now when this fool came to borrow a soup saying his girl hasn't had time to put money on his books, I had just given Meeka two stacks to pay some shit off. I hope and pray she not giving this fool my money on the low. Sure as my name is Turk, I would \snuff that hoe off faster than she can tie her shoes. It's all coming into view now. I bet that cat had something to do with me being attacked in the shower a while back. These bitches were trying to kill me, but I was too smart for them. Shit keeps adding up. I thanked my man and signal the guard to let me back in the pod. I had to strategize my plans. First, devising a plan on how I was going to fuck T-Rock up. Secondly, handling Meeka's dumb ass, and finally how I could seduce Ms. O'Conner into giving up the ass.

I had to plan smart, making sure everything that was about to go down didn't lead back and incriminate me. I'll start with Meeka, she won't see this shit coming from a mile away. The bitch so money hungry and greedy she'll think she hit the jackpot. I made a few calls from my throw-away phone I had hidden in my property. Set everything up from who, what, when, where, and how to go about handling things. It was going down sooner than later, all I had to do was give the word. I then went about my normal activities. Since I had already made arrangements to handle the two thorns in my side, it was now time I made an appointment to see my sexy chocolate. Pushing the button on the intercom system, the guard answered up. I let him know I would need about four more requests for service forms and I would be missing dinner. The guard acknowledged my request and then he closed the door to my cell.

Shortly after the dinner hour, I walked up to the front of the dayroom area and handed the guard my request forms to place in the box for me, then I walked back to my cell. This time I checked my phone for any messages and to give word to go forward with the plan. I was known for sending Meeka flowers, candy, balloons, and nice, expensive gifts. A dozen long stem pink roses were to arrive at our house along with a four-carat diamond tennis bracelet and an American Express pre-paid gift card with a thousand stacks on it. Little did she know, she wouldn't receive any of the gifts and the person delivering it was going to knock her off. I gave them instructions to make it seem like a burglary gone badly. As for fuck boy who begs for soups, I plan on handling him myself.

I had to choose the perfect time to handle this other subject. The timing had to be just right. He would never suspect a thing and would totally be caught off guard. The next morning, I went to the prison infirmary complaining of stomach issues and chest pains. This would give me time to establish an alibi. The nurses and doctors examined me and decided I would be temporarily housed in the hospital ward for observation. I had paid some of the CO's off a while back; they owed me a favor. They allowed me to sneak out of the ward and I made my move. I knew the night shift guards working my pod would be sleep during the 0100-0245 hours. Using the keys I obtained from the other guards, I went through the side entrance and made my way inside. Everyone was sleep except for a few of my homies who were already aware of what was about to transpire. Making my way to T-Rock's cell, I gently opened his door and stepped inside. He was asleep.

I pulled a plastic bag, a roll of gauze, and a syringe out of my pants and commence to committing my crime. I strangled him, and then stuffed his mouth with the gauze. Once the life was choked out of him, I stuck the syringe into his neck for the final kill. The medication inside of that syringe had the same ingredients used for those on death row. When finished, I made my way back to the hospital ward and slept like a baby.

Later on that night, the guards found T-Rock's body while making their rounds. The prison was on lock down. They didn't have a clue what happened to him. No one knew.

The following day, Ms. O'Conner came to pay me a visit and tell me everything was looking good for my release. She asked me how I was feeling and I responded by saying, "I could be better, but now that I see you I feel great." I told Ms. O'Conner once they released me from medical I would pay her another visit.

She winked at me and said, "Okay."

That was my cue to put this entire dick on her. She wanted me just as badly as I was yearning for her. I quickly found some request forms and turned them in so I could make an appointment with her. As long as I had an appointment, the activities that were about to go down wouldn't seem the least bit suspicious.

*** 

Sandra O'Conner

"Not sure what just happened during my visit with inmate Rollins, but this man makes my pussy tingle in all sorts of ways. Why did I wink my eye at him as I was leaving? Something has come over me when it comes to this inmate. I have never in my fifteen years of working in this field found any of my clients attractive nor have I been sexually attractive to them. However, this one makes me want to skip and do flips with him. I know I could lose my job and everything I own, but I've convinced myself trying him one time couldn't hurt. Could it?" I said, in deep thought.

While sitting in my office, I begin running all types of background checks on Mr. Turk Rollins. Needed to see exactly what type of individual he was. I had to see what type of person had captured interest and could possibly put my career on the line. When I completed my research, I was pleased to see that the most he had ever been charged with was attempt to manufacture and deliver. I could live with that. And he didn't even realize while he was lying in that hospital bed that I saw every inch of his dick print and it caused my body to convulse internally. He had piqued my interest and now my body ached to feel him deep inside. The imprint his dick made through that hospital gown he had on made my eyes buck almost completely out of my head. I had to maintain my composure and stay professional, but once I returned to my office, I closed the door, locked it, turned on my CD player where New Edition was wondering if we can stand the rain and R. Kelly was giving instructions on his "12 Play". The music had me in a zone and I began playing with my pussy until I exploded all over myself. The shit seemed so unreal. Never in a million years had I ever expected to fall for an inmate. Maybe it's a dream and I'll wake up soon. If not, I knew what I was about to do was playing with fire and I could possibly get burned.

The next day, I arrived to work and noticed Mr. Rollins had put in a request to come to my office. I had taken a few extra minutes preparing myself at home before coming to work. I had used my seductive smelling perfume, and put on a fitted skirt with no panties. Today, I would see what Mr. Rollins and his dick had to offer. I should put up more of a fight, but seeing how I haven't had a man inside these thighs in months, I need this right about now, I thought. I'm going to do this one time, then I had to stop. If he kept sending me requests to come to my office, I would have to turn him away. Don't need the both of us getting caught up with this prison love affair.

*** 

## Turk Rollins

Around 2:30 p.m. the next day, I received word that I had been approved for my appointment. Having been up all night preparing for this day, I made sure I had my game strategy planned out. There wouldn't be much talking once I entered Ms. O'Conner's office and my dick would soon be so deep in her pussy, we were both going to feel like we were on Mars. She would enjoy every inch that this dick had to offer. I'm going to make sure of that. Just a matter of time and it would fall in place.

The guard escorted me from the infirmary down the corridor to Ms. O'Conner's office. It's the same routine day in and day out. When you're locked up, you kind of get used to it. The pat searches, the shake down of the cells, being escorted to and from all offices in the building. Shortly after arriving in front of Ms. O'Conner's door, she opened it and gestured for me to come in. The fragrance this woman was wearing had all parts of my body twitching, turning, and aroused in ways I'd never experienced before. I noticed how form-fitting her skirt was and didn't see any panty lines, so she either had on a thong or wasn't wearing any. I'm not here for any small talk so I had better move in for the kill, I thought.

"Mmm, that's some nice smelling perfume you have on, Ms. O'Conner. May I ask what it is you're wearing that has my nose open like a faucet?"

"It's called Burberry Brit for Women. Do you like?" Ms. O'Conner asked.

"Yes, ma'am, I do. I like more than just the perfume you have on. I like the way you're wearing that skirt, the bun you have in your hair, the fullness of your lips that I'm dying to kiss. I like the way you walk, talk, and sit. I like everything I see. You're beauty at its best," Rollins catechized.

\*\*\*

Sandra O'Conner

Rollins walked from around the desk area and stood within inches of me. He spoke softly, "You know you feel this attraction between us and I don't need any info about my parole. I already know everything is handled on my behalf. However, I am interested in you and what you have between them thighs. I can feel the heat from over here, so stop the act and let's do what we both know we want to do and be done with it."

Before I could reply, he moved in a little closer and kissed me long and deep. His tongue swirled around in my mouth in ways I had only seen on television. The way he bit my bottom lip and sucked on the top all while deep throating me with his long, thick, moist tongue, had me falling on the floor. I was so enthralled by this affection. He was now standing so close to me, I could feel the bulge in his pants on my thigh and I began to get wet. Before I knew it, he had picked me up with one arm and was moving stuff off my desk with the other. He then placed me on my back and hiked up my skirt.

"Aww, just as I figured, you don't have any panties on. You knew what was going down when I came in today.

Look how pretty this pussy looks and how wet it is. Oh my God, baby, you just lay there. I got this," Rollins screeched.

Rollins had me at the edge of my desk, where he could have easy access to me. He started fingering my pussy with one hand and caressing my breasts with the other. In a single stroke, he had his hand up in my pussy. I could feel the orgasm building up inside me. Next thing I knew, he had his head between my thighs kissing every inch of me. He opened up the labia of my pussy and started to lick and suck. Fast and slow then he repeated the action. My head started spinning. I couldn't catch my breath. He flipped me over and told me to hike my ass in the air. He climbed on top of my desk, pulled his pants down, and rammed his thick, long dick up in my pussy. The juices started running down my leg and he kept pounding every inch in and out. Just when I thought he was about to cum, he stopped and stood up. "Come give me some head so I can nut," he insisted.

At this point, I didn't mind. I felt this big muscle mass inside me and I wanted to taste it as well. I had never sucked a dick this size before so I hoped I could take it all in. I started at the tip and the more I took in, he began pumping his hips and holding the back of my head. I was enjoying every minute of this. Then there was a knock at the door.

"Ms. O'Conner, I have some packages for you," the voice from the other side of the door said.

"Just leave them on the ground, I'll get them shortly," I responded. "Whoosh, that was close!"

"You don't think we're done, do you, Ms. O'Conner?" Rollins asked.

"Well, yes. I have to get back to work," I said.

"Well we aren't done by far. I haven't busted my nut and as good as this pussy tasted and the wetness was feeling on my dick, you got one or two choices. You either going to suck me off, or I'm driving this dick in your ass as deep as I can get it. Now which one you choose?" Rollins barked.

I had never done anal sex before, but I was willing to try it, just not at this moment. So, I got down on my knees and began sucking and stroking his dick once again. He pumped his hips and grabbed the back of my hair. He had his dick so far down my throat it made it hard to breathe, swallow, and concentrate. I started to choke. Just as he gave one more pump into my mouth, he let out a grunt. Then I felt the warm liquid flow out the sides of my mouth and down my throat.

"You have got to go now before anyone suspects anything," I said frantically, while pulling my skirt down and fixing my hair. I was nervous and overwhelmed all at the same time. I didn't know what to do at this point but I knew I wanted to hook up with this dude once again. I longed for him and needed him to fulfill my sexual desire, even if it was under the most unacceptable manner there was. I just needed to be a little more careful next time so no one would come knocking on the door looking for me. I looked over at Rollins and he had this devilish smirk on his face.

"What's so funny?" I asked.

"You are," he replied.

A puzzled look came over my face. "What do you mean, I am?"

"Look, Ma, you knew what you were getting yourself into when you dressed the way you did before coming to work. You not wearing any panties, that tight-fitting skirt, the special perfume you chose, and the way you wore your hair. You also knew that this situation was going to occur because you wanted it just as much as I did. Don't sit here and act like you're in shock or surprised that someone was knocking on the door. It's a chance you took and obviously was more than willing to partake in. Then to top it all off, you know I'm locked up and you never once had a concern about a condom. You let me go raw all up in you. Where do you think the nut went beside that you swallowed it?" Rollins smirked.

Knowing he was right, I still didn't want it thrown in my face, so I became angry. I began yelling at him. "Get the fuck out of my office. Right now, Rollins!" I knew someone would knock on the door again and ask if everything was okay. That's exactly what I wanted to happen.

Soon a knock came at the door. "Is everything alright in there?" the voice from the other side inquired.

I swung the door wide open. "Yes, everything is just fine. This inmate was just leaving," I assured.

Rollins looked me in the eyes as he was leaving and said, "This ain't over."

After a half hour or so had passed, I began cleaning my office. All the items Rollins had thrown on the floor before placing me on top of my desk were scattered everywhere. Each moment, I kept reliving the events that had taken place in this space. The way he touched me, the caress of his hand, his lips as they pressed against my body.

The suspense of being involved with him and not getting caught. It was a real adrenaline rush. In my mind, I was ready to do it all over again, but I knew it was too much of a risk. Oh, hell I'm already in too deep. He could use this against me at any time. All he had to do was put in a kite to any of the supervisors here and I'd be fired. So I guess he has the upper hand at the moment.

Several days went by and I hadn't heard from Rollins, which really surprised me. The unit was on lockdown due to an investigation that was taking place. I'm not sure what happened, but from my understanding, someone had been found dead several days ago, in the same housing unit as Rollins. He never made mention that something happened, or maybe he wasn't aware since he was still assigned to the infirmary unit. That entire day, all I could think about was Rollins. I didn't get much work done from being worried something terrible had happened to him. I didn't want to draw attention to myself by inquiring about him, but I needed to know if he was alright. I called down to cell block twenty-seven and asked the guard who answered the phone what was going on.

He responded, "We found an inmate named Terrence Higgins. The inmates call him T-Rock. He was unresponsive and his throat was sliced a few days ago. No one seems to know what happened to him, but it has foul play written all over it. He is a known thief, so maybe someone got their revenge."

I thanked the guard for his time and hung up. A sigh of relief came over me. I was glad nothing bad had happened to Rollins.

Several more days went by and IAD (Internal Affairs Division) finished their investigation and didn't have a suspect or even know where to begin. They deemed this death a retaliation homicide and said they would keep their eyes and ears open if anyone knows anything. Basically, they swept this under the rug so they wouldn't draw attention to the confinement bureau.

My work day ended and I headed home. When I arrived, I checked the mailbox and watered the flowers before entering the house. When I finished outside, I entered the house and decided to flip through the mail. There was a package with no return address listed on it. I became skeptical about opening it, but curiosity made me do so anyways. Inside of the envelope was a note and a diamond necklace with a heart shaped pendant. Suspicions of who sent these items made me skeptical about reading what the note had to say. I went into the kitchen and poured a glass of wine, then went into the master bath and ran some hot bath water to help me relax. As the water filled the tub, I turned on some relaxing jazz music and lit a few candles. Once the water was the correct temperature, I got undressed and submerged my aching body into the water. I must have been in there for hours, because before I knew it, my cell phone was ringing. It was from an unknown number. Reaching over the side of the tub, I answered the phone. "Hello?"

No one said anything.

"Hello, is there anyone there?" Still nothing. Then the phone went dead. Hmm must have been a wrong number. Checking the clock to see what time it was, I decided it was time for me to get dressed so I could prepare dinner.

Looking through items in the closet, I chose a pair of booty shorts and a tank top. I picked up the mail that I'd placed on the table prior and headed into the kitchen. Tonight, I would make something simple since I was extremely tired and just wanted to go to bed, but knew I needed to eat. Opening the refrigerator door, I noticed I had taken out boneless chicken breasts, so I decided to boil noodles and make a quick chicken Alfredo. I diced up a few tomatoes and found some spinach, then poured me another glass of wine and sat down to read the mail. The suspicious package still had me wondering who could have sent it. I decided to read the note that came with it.

Hello Sandra, I hope this package shows a small token of my gratitude and appreciation for you. I know things didn't end as well as we both would have like the other day, but I didn't want to seem as if I had taken advantage of you. Please accept this necklace as a peace offering. I want to see you again before I parole out of here. You're sexy, smart, and beautiful. Spending as much time as possible with you means the world to me. You're all I think about when I lay down at night and the first thing that comes to mind when I rise. As you know, my cell block has been on lock down due to someone dying. I put in a request to come to your office tomorrow so be expecting me, because I sure will be expecting you. Well, I have to go for now. Until we see each other again.

Respectfully, Turk put the note on the countertop, my jaw dropped in disbelief. How in the hell did he get my address, let alone know my first name? I never told him anything about my personal life, so how is it he has this information about me? What the hell was really going on? I hoped he didn't send this as a hush gift. I see I'm going to have to put my foot down if he is. There was a feeling of absence the last few days since I hadn't had an opportunity to visit or see Rollins. My body had been yearning with desire to partake of his lust one more time. After scrolling through the remainder of the mail and washing the dishes, I turned in early. Having decided I would go in early to finish some paperwork and sign some papers for several others that were being released that day.

I planned on seeing Mr. Turk Rollins early, that way I would have the rest of the day to myself.

The alarm went off around 4:30 the next morning. Dreadful about being up this early, I made my way into the bathroom to freshen up. My clothes were already laid out for me to put on. It took me approximately twenty minutes to get ready and out the door.

Driving in, I began listening to Steve Harvey on the radio for my morning inspiration. I arrived at work around 5:30 a.m. and headed straight to my office. Once there, I sorted through all my paperwork and prioritized it by release dates. I checked my inbox, and sure enough Rollins had put in several requests to come to my office. I couldn't allow his requests to detour me from my work, so I quickly got busy on the other important items. Seemed like I worked an entire shift by time the other employees had arrived. As I reviewed the release papers, Turk's caught my attention. He would be released in the next couple of days.

The name of the person he was being released to also caught my eye. The name seemed awfully familiar. I set it to the side. The clock on my desk started beeping at 9:15 a.m. Let me notify the guard on duty down on the block to send Rollins to my office.

Several moments later there was a knock at my door. Already having an idea of who was on the other side, I simply said, "Come in."

Turk entered my office with a smile as big as the moon, closing the door behind him. "Did you get the little gift I sent you? Did you like it? I had it specially made just for you."

"Yes, I did," I replied as I jumped from my seat and

wrapped my arms around his neck, then began kissing those lovely lips I missed so much.

He gripped my ass and started massaging it with his hands. His tongue did dances inside my mouth like they were dancing to a beat. He pulled away. "Turn over. Let me see that ass for a second. My, my not wearing any panties again today I see," Turk said.

He bent me over the chair, hiked up my skirt, and began rubbing the head of his dick on my ass. Instant wetness from my pussy started to flow. "You like this dick on your ass, huh? I want to feel this dick all up in that hot, wet pussy. Then I want you to cum all over it like you did the last time, except this time we don't have to rush."

In a whisper, I replied, "Okay."

Turk teased me by putting just the head of his dick inside my pussy and pulling it out. He did this for several strokes before he rammed it deep inside of me. He cupped my breasts with both hands as we grinded together and sweat poured from our bodies. This was all wrong but felt oh so good.

We both climaxed at the same time and I was spent. It took me several minutes to compose myself. After I had collected myself, I gave him the news about his release. He didn't seem too happy about going home.

"Is there a problem, Turk? This should be some great news for you but you don't seem the least bit happy."

"I am, Ma. Don't worry, I am," he replied.

Over the next few days, Turk and I met in my office and had our fuck sessions. On the day of his release, he paid me one last visit and gave me a good fucking before he left. He told me he would contact me in a few days once he was settled in his place. I was sad to see Turk go, but happy he was going to be free. Then it dawned on me. Those papers and the name on it kept bothering me, so I did some research to find out why the name sounded so familiar. Running the name through the national database, a headline popped up: Tameeka Reynolds, age 25 found dead. It stated she was pregnant at the time of her death. How could he be getting paroled to her address and she was deceased? It was none of my business, but it just didn't sit well with me.

Several days later, Turk contacted me just like he said he would. He came over late one night and we had even wilder sex than we did in my office. We ended up falling asleep in each other's arms. When I woke up the next morning he was gone. He left a note on the nightstand with six crispy one hundred dollar bills.

Morning babe,
Didn't want to wake you. I had business to attend to. Here, take this money and go buy yourself something nice. I'll see you later on night. Turk. I couldn't stop smiling to save my life. I rolled back over for a few more hours before deciding to get up and start my day. Walking by the calendar on the wall, I noticed I was two weeks late for my period. Maybe it was the stress from the job and all the things I had been doing. I guess while I'm out, I'll stop by the pharmacy and grab a pregnancy test just to make sure.

After running errands and grabbing groceries to cook, I ran bath water and decided I would take the pregnancy test then. The water was just the right temperature, so I began to get undressed. I noticed my breasts were a slight bit tender. Following the directions on the package, I peed in this little cup, then took the bulb and dropped a dot of pee on the test strip. It didn't take much time before the double lines showed up. Oh, my God, it's positive. What am I going to do? I thought. What the hell am I going to tell Turk? Even if I decided to keep this baby, what would I tell my co-workers? "Oh, I'm pregnant by an ex-con?" I had a lot to think about and decisions to make. And only a short time to do it.

About 7:30 in the evening, there was a knock at the door. It was Turk. "Murder She Wrote" was on the television, so I must have drifted off to sleep. I opened the door and allowed him to come in. He greeted me with a passionate kiss on the lips. Tears instantly started flowing down my cheeks.

"What's wrong, baby? Did something happen while I was gone?"

Choked up from crying, I mumbled, "I'm pregnant! What are we going to do?"

Turk turned to me and smiled. "Everything is going to be alright, my love. Just let me do what I need to do and you'll have nothing to worry about."

I wanted to believe him, but I still had to deal with the fact that, if my job found out I messed with a convicted criminal, I could get fired. That part scared me to death. Weeks went by, and I decided I was going to keep this baby. Turk had moved in, and even though he would be gone most of the day, he made sure he was home every night to hold me tight as I slept. Since moving in, we've had more love sessions, and each time it was more passionate and intense. He made sure all my needs were met, not leaving one unattended. He made me feel secure and safe. I knew questions would start flowing at my job the bigger my belly got. I would just make up a lie about being artificially inseminated. Everyone knew how much I had always wanted a baby. I just didn't want one under this type of circumstance.

Over the next several months, my belly grew like green beans. It began to poke out a little bit and everyone complimented me on my baby bump. Turk and I were returning home from my five-month checkup. We had only been in the house approximately fifteen minutes before someone was beating down the door. Neither of us was expecting company so I yelled, "Who is it?"

"It's the police. Open the door now!" one of the officers yelled.

Turk and I looked at each other in disbelief at the actions taking place. He kissed me on the forehead and said, "Baby, I'm going to miss you, I'm sorry."

At this time, the police burst through the door yelling and screaming, "Everybody get down. Get down now and put your hands on top of your head." I'm clueless as to why the police just busted down my door. Tears were streaming down my face and all I could hear were officers yelling directions. "I'm pregnant!" I screamed back.

"Turk Rollins, you are under arrest for the murder of Tameeka Reynolds and for the possession and attempted delivery of a control substance. Do you understand?" the arresting officer barked.

"What the hell is going on? Turk, what are they talking about, baby? Murder?"
"Baby, call my lawyer. We will work all this out. There must be a misunderstanding or something."

Just when I thought I had it all worked out, shit backfired

in my face. Turk was looking at twenty-five to life for the murder charge and an additional twenty for the drugs. My job found out Turk was living with me at the time of his arrest and put two and two together and figured out that's who I must be pregnant by. They fired me the next day following their investigation. I should have seen it coming. Shit was going too good. Every day, I asked myself: how did I go from accepting a new position with my employer to having casual sex with an inmate while he was locked up? To now being pregnant by him and having him live in my house? They always say when you play with fire you eventually get burned.

# CLOSURE

My body is here with you, but my heart is with him

But I just wanna devour you limb from limb

We reminisce about how wild we were back then

And how you never wanted more than to simply be fuck friends

It's like magic used to happen when we got together

Now a story must end that should have lasted forever

Now that time has passed, you see I'm a good catch

As I touch you I'm thinking we definitely would've matched

But I couldn't wait for you the rest of my life

So, I told him, "Yes I will be your wife."

And it's sad but you have to respect it

It's tough, but you should've expected it

'Cause you had me in your arms, but commitment was rejected

I guess I felt unaccepted, my worth felt under rated

So I went and found a man who could better appreciate it
But, tonight I'm next to you for one last time

To give closure to a love that wasn't worth a dime

So, I'm fucking away the pain and sucking away the sorrow

We are literally fucking like there is no tomorrow

So this is my last kiss, this is your last lick

I take a mental picture like, "Damn, that dick thick."

And, when it's all over we say goodbye and smile

Now wish me the best tomorrow when I walk down that aisle.

# *TANGLED WEB*

My radio was playing The Beat 97.9 FM in my bedroom, and one of my all-time favorite songs comes on the station. Leela James "Fall for You". I can't help but to sing along. This song is powerful and has deep emotional meaning
.

"Here we are, together
And everything between us is good
I'm right here in this cloud, baby
Ready to fly, but before I take
Another step
Would you catch me if I fall for you?
'Cause I'm falling
I'm falling, I'm falling."

By time the song finished on the radio, my face was drenched with tears. Ever since the first time I heard this song at a party it touched me. This song sends a deeply embedded message to me that love isn't far-fetched, you just have to be willing to open up and accept it. I haven't had much luck in the love department. There always seems to be some underlying situation that blows up in my face sooner or later.

I'm Monica Lewis, 26 years old, a college graduate of Louisiana State University, currently residing in Dallas, TX and employed with AT&T as an IT Specialist. Over the course of the last five years, I've been in several different relationships, but this last encounter ended, leaving a permanent mark.

While in college, I dated several guys. None of whom were suitable enough to have a serious, committed relationship with. Most of these guys were just a romp in the hay and see you the next day type of dudes. During my sophomore year, there was this one guy, Justin, who I thought was special, had developed some feelings for, and considered being monogamous with, that cheated on me with several of the girls on the flag team. Come to find out, he had been seeing each of them for months and I never knew. He made a total fool out of me. I was devastated, emotional, and a total wreck. My world was caving in and I didn't know if I was coming or going.

I vowed from that day forward to never be that vulnerable again. Not only did this guy cheat on me, he spread vicious rumors about me across campus. He told everyone that he and his buddies had run trains on me repeatedly and that I was easy. He photoshopped pictures of me engaging in such acts, and made posters with disgusting comments about me on them. My closest of friends, who knew me well, even looked at me funny. This type of disrespect would not happen again under any circumstances if I had any say so in the matter.

People on the campus never forgot about the situation with Justin and how he embarrassed and dehumanized me. When I would walk across the campus, I would get all types of people staring at me. In the beginning, I would miss class and stay confined in my room. I would only go out when it was dark and that's if I absolutely had to. Too ashamed about the incident, I hide myself in the dorm, unable to show my face or go about my daily activities as usual. My so-called friends were no longer my friends. They didn't want to be associated with someone who was labeled a whore.

It took months, but by the time the summer of my junior year rolled around everything had settled down enough that I wasn't afraid of going out during the day. That semester had ushered in a different crowd and none of them seemed interested in the antics of campus gossip. Some of the friends who deserted me during my hard times had started coming back around. Things could never be the same, but it was good to have people to hang out with from time to time.

Having accepted what had happened to me, I tried to start over and put the past behind me. I knew I wasn't innocent by far and had committed some sex acts many would be ashamed of. I've had threesomes, sex with women, oral and anal sex, and sex with multiple partners in one day. Sex with toys was my all-time favorite. It's my personal belief that whatever I did with someone was my business, not that of everyone else. That incident was a learning experience. Can't trust everyone and everyone isn't my friend. Coming to grips with the reality of the humiliation, struggling to maintain my grades in class, and being emotionally drained was taking a toll on me. My professors worked with me on my assignments. They knew if I wasn't in class that day it must have been a bad day. They were glad when I did attend class because they knew they could call on me to answer questions over the reading assignment and homework.

My friends around me always tried to motivate me and encourage me to seek counseling, to speak out, or pray about my situation. They constantly told me the pity party I was throwing for myself wasn't a good look. The feeling of being trapped, not only inside my own body, but actually inside my dorm room had gotten to me. I had come to the conclusion I could no longer play the victim and had to get over it. Finally, things had boiled over enough that they were somewhat back to normal. My grades were getting much better since I had devoted more time to study. Isolation gives you the opportunity to really get to know yourself. I was glad my head was back on track and I could move forward.

Over the course of the next several months after graduation, I gave dating another try. Seeing how my last encounter wasn't the best, I was a little standoffish. Didn't really know what to expect out of this, but I promised myself I would remain open-minded. I knew I couldn't let my past prohibit me from moving forward in my future. I met Monroe at the local 7-eleven store while I was getting gas. He introduced himself and told me how beautiful I looked. We exchanged names and he asked if he could take me out sometime. Feeling awkward, I brushed his advances off. He noticed and told me I could pick wherever I wanted to go and he would be okay with it. We did something simple for the first date. Monroe took me miniature golfing and to the pizza parlor to eat. It felt good to dress up instead of wearing the normal sweat pants and T-shirt. I enjoyed being out amongst others like me. It felt great. Before parting ways, Monroe kissed me on my forehead then walked me to my car.

The forehead kiss was a sign of respect and endearment. Means the individual sees you as more than a sexual object, they value you as a person.

Monroe and I went on several more dates. We were really getting to know one another. I was still in shock from the way we parted the last few times. Each time Monroe kissed me on my forehead, I desperately wanted him to kiss my lips. Feeling unwanted and not understanding the concept of the forehead kiss, I turned to my roommate for some input on what she thought about it. She informed me of the natural meaning behind it and how it is a sign of sincerity and respect. She then went into details of what each kiss meant by relationship definitions.

She sent me to a website that talked about the different attributes of a kiss. It defined the amorous reflection of how each kiss is viewed. First on the list was the forehead kiss: We're cute together. The next one, the kiss on the cheek: We're friends. The kiss on the hand: I adore you. Kiss on the neck: I want you, now. Kiss on the shoulder: You're perfect. And the kiss on the lips: I love you. After having all of this explained to me, I knew Monroe wasn't ready to express his love, so the forehead kiss was the next best thing. It was gentle and kind. It was admirable, I could actually get used to this.

On our next date, I asked Monroe what he thought about relationships and events from a person's past interfering in them. Monroe replied, "A foundation to any relationship begins with being friends and having trust. If you don't have trust, communication, dedication, to be equally yoked, and a basic sense of understanding to help build the foundation, then whatever type of relationship you're trying to have doesn't have stability."

Monroe in turn asked me, "Are you spiritual?"

Answering him as honest as I knew how, I said, "Yes, I believe in a Higher Power. I believe that there is someone who sits high and looks low and hears my humble cries."

He then looked at me and spoke once again. "Then you know when you pray you're supposed to ask God, Jehovah, Yahweh, or whatever title you give Him. You're supposed to ask Him to heal you from whatever is troubling you inside. You ask for forgiveness not just for those who have betrayed you but for yourself as well. That's the only way the healing process can begin."

You know, he was absolutely right. I'd been holding all of this anger and frustration inside. I knew he could probably sense it from a mile away. The bumptious behavior I had been displaying was rude and uncalled for. Monroe remained calm and peaceful regardless of my insensitive actions. He could somehow sense my actions were more pugnacious than anything and I could be fixed. He was teaching me to love myself and to forgive. He was healing wounds and opening doors I didn't realize existed. He was pulling me out of the tangled web I was once in, making me whole again.

My spirit was heavy. It felt like that of a broken vessel. Never in a million years would I have thought anyone would want me ever again. Fearing if I told Monroe the details of what happened to me while in college, he would never forgive me. The fear of coming off selfish or feeling as if I were keeping a secret was eating me alive. Unable to hold it in any longer, I decided to inform him of the mess I was involved in.

After hearing my story and watching the tears flow down my face, Monroe took me into his embrace and held me tight. He gently placed a kiss on my forehead, letting me know everything would be alright. It was something about this kiss that was different from the rest. It burned through me into my soul, sending sparks and shock waves into places it's never gone before. My body tingled all over. Monroe continued to pull me in with a passionate desire.

"I have a confession," Monroe whispered.

"What is it? You know you can tell me anything," I replied.

"I've always known about you, Monica. I've known since the first day I saw you at the 7-eleven. I already knew who you were. To you, I've always been this invisible being. I've seen you across campus many times before and not once would you give me the time of day. You didn't give the slightest acknowledgement or say hi. Even after the horrible things those guys did to you. I tried to reach out to you by sending you messages and flowers. You blew me off. I was never doubtful about meeting you. I even prayed that one day you would find in your heart to see me as a person and allow me to pamper you and show you how to love. That life goes on even in the darkest of night. I carry a deep desire for you, and I had to find a way to let you know, you were not alone. You have someone."

In the back of my mind I was thinking, I hope this guy isn't some pervert, serial rapist, or stalker.

Many questions raced through my head. I often wondered why someone would knowingly want to give me the benefit of a doubt, knowing what my past entailed. Questioning myself repeatedly, I had to remind myself that I wasn't perfect and was entitled to makes mistakes. I needed to get a grip on who I was and focus on moving forward. I'm thankful for Monroe and his consistent efforts. He is a great man whom I'm glad to know.

To help get me out of this funk I was in, Monroe had planned a romantic evening for us. He invited me over to his place. He instructed me to wear something sexy, but elegant. Monroe told me he wanted me as dolled up as if

we were spending a night out on the town. Not really knowing what to expect, I ran a hot bubble bath, where I soaked my tired body, allowing the water to relax me and the scented fragrance of the bath oils to stimulate my senses. After about an hour or so of being submerged in the water, my skin began to shrivel and shrink. The water had turned cold, so I knew it was now time to get out.

Once out of the tub, I dried myself off with the cotton Egyptian towels. While still a little damp, I sprayed on my Vera Wang perfume. Then I used some baby oil and rubbed down my entire body, placed powder on my breasts, and plugged in my curlers to do my hair. On the bed, I had already placed an all-black, spaghetti strapped, form fitting dress. Matching black lace panties and bra lay beside it. Still, I was unsure of what footwear I was going to choose. I decided that would be the last thing I did after getting myself prepared.

My hair was pinned up with bobby pins and I looked at myself in the mirror. I couldn't believe who the person was that was looking back at me. She was radiant and beautiful, full of life, and deserving of this evening. Waiting a few minutes for all the excitement to sink in, I applied my makeup, and then I tested the curlers to make sure they were hot enough. I used the curlers to make big curls all over my entire head. When finished, I brushed my hair into an up-do and left the sides hang in S-curl patterns. It was time to put my dress on. Before leaving my apartment, I phoned Monroe to let him know I was on my way. He notified me he would pick me up and to just hold tight for a moment.

When Monroe arrived, he handed me six long stemmed assorted roses and a box of chocolate. "You look absolutely amazing," he said.

The flowers he brought smelled wonderful. Leaning in to give Monroe a hug, he welcomed me with open arms. Monroe complimented me on my perfume. "Hmm, you smell delightful."

"Thank you, Monroe. I appreciate the compliment," I responded.

We embraced. He pulled back for just a second to admire me again. Monroe leaned in again, this time planting a succulent wet kiss on my lips. Our tongues began to dance, and soon became knotted up like a pretzel. The extreme intensity left me breathless. This kiss was full of compassion, desire, and lust. Monroe had me melting in his arms at that very moment.

We left my apartment and Monroe drove us to his place. Once we pulled into the driveway, he parked the car, then got out and walked around to the passenger side to open the door for me. He took my hand and guided me to the front door. Monroe turned to me and said, "I need for you to close your eyes and trust me. I'm going to put this blindfold on you and once inside I will remove it."

Shaking my head in agreement, I responded, "Okay, I will."

Monroe placed the blindfold around my eyes and tied it gently at the back of my head. "Remember, trust me. I won't do anything to cause you any harm."

I could hear Monroe jiggling his keys to open the door. Once the door was opened, I didn't hear anything. There was pure silence. My heart began racing, anticipating what the big secret was he had in store for me. We walked further into his place. The fresh scent of lavender, vanilla, and apple spice filled the air. Suddenly, I became nervous. Opening my mouth to speak, no words seemed to come forward.

"Relax, my love. You can take the blindfold off now. I told you I wouldn't do anything to harm you," Monroe expressed.

Hurriedly, I yanked the blindfold from around my eyes. What I saw in front of me was unbelievable. There were candles lit all around, the dinner table was delicately set for two, there was wine poured into the wine glasses, and on a dinner cart next to it was our meal. Romantic music quietly played in the background.

Marvin Gaye was bellowing away one of my favorite tunes, "Sexual Healing". The music was indeed a mood setter. Monroe guided me with one hand, and with the other, he pulled out my chair for me to sit. Once seated, he rolled the cart with our food over to me, took the lid off the dish displaying lobster tails, shrimp, and scallops. He had also prepared whole asparagus, potatoes, and dinner rolls.

"I hope you don't mind if we eat by candle light. I want this night to be as romantic as possible," he stated.

Nervously I responded, "I love everything about this evening already. I don't mind."

During dinner, we talked, laughed, and I even shed a tear or two. We were open with one another, sharing information about our feelings for one another. We both were enjoying this romantic evening and all that it had to offer. Monroe expressed his deepest feelings and I expressed mine. This would definitely be a night to remember. After we finished at the dinner table, we made our way into the living room and sat on the couch. We continued to talk and talking turned into kissing and kissing turned into hot, vivid, and passionate foreplay.

This man was driving the inner beast in me. My body temperature must have risen at least ten degrees. The tantalizing kisses he was planting on me turned on my inner freak. I was ready for some action and I needed it now. My pussy was hungry, my clit was throbbing, and my juices had begun to flow.

My sexual desire was at an all-time high. I just hoped I didn't give the wrong impression.

"Are you alright, my love? I'm not making you uncomfortable, am I?" Monroe inquired.

"No, everything's just fine. I'm okay, but I must be honest. I want you more than I have ever wanted anyone in my entire life. I just don't want to give you the wrong impression," I explained.

"Baby, you could never give me the wrong impression. I've already told you I've always had an attraction to you and there is nothing you do that would interfere with the way I feel about you," Monroe recounted.

At that moment, Monroe rose from the couch, grabbed me by my hand, and guided me to the private sanctuary of his room. More candles were lit. Rose pedals were placed on the bed, plastic was laid out on the floor, a bottle of champagne was in a bucket of ice on the nightstand, and R. Kelly was crooning his seductive "12 Play" hits. Standing behind me, Monroe unzipped my dress and allowed it to fall to the floor. He then unhooked my bra and assisted me out of my panties.

"Lie down on the bed while I get prepared. This is a night I have been waiting on for such a long time," Monroe uttered.

Doing as I was told, I watched Monroe undress himself in my presence. His manhood was standing at attention and the look in his eyes was devilish. Whatever he had in store for this night, I could tell it was going to be mind-blowing.

As I lay on the bed, the silhouette from the candles painted a pretty picture. My mind was racing, heart was beating fast, and my body was tingling all over. Monroe walked over to the bed and started to caress my feet, legs, and thighs until he had touched my entire body. After the massage, he kissed every inch of me with the most tender kisses a man could give a woman. Felt as if I was in heaven.

We kissed some more and his touches were more rampant and determined. He spread my legs and massaged my clit, fingered my pussy, and teased my tongue all at the same time.

"Come lie on the floor and let me explore every inch of you in a way I know you desire. We are going to do something tonight that will leave an everlasting imprint on your mind," Monroe expressed.

All I could do was look at him with tear stained eyes and prepare to enjoy whatever he had planned for me. I got myself off the bed and lay down on the plastic he had placed on the floor. He assisted me down on the floor and stood over me. I closed my eyes to take in everything that was about to happen. The music was changing from one song to the next and the mood was perfectly set. The more Monroe touched and caressed and kissed me, the more I wanted him to just take me and do as he pleased.

Monroe took the bottle of champagne and poured some of it on my naked body. He slurped and sucked every crevice of my body, sucking up the champagne. He then took a few ice cubes from the bucket, spread my legs, and rubbed my clit with several of the cubes.

Once he had stimulated my clit he began sucking, licking, and teasing my pussy in ways that brought great pleasure. He then stood above me and rained down golden showers of piss all over my body. The only thing I could think of was R. Kelly had really gotten ahold of this man. After relieving himself all over me, Monroe took a warm, wet, soapy hand towel and cleaned me up.

"Turn over, baby. I want to see this ass hiked up in the air," Monroe muttered.

As I turned over, Monroe slapped my ass with full force. It sent electrifying impulses throughout my entire body. It was a pain that could not be described, but it hurt so good. With one smooth rip he opened a golden sealed package that he had retrieved from the dresser. Without interrupting what he was doing, he placed the condom on his fully erect dick.

He then mounted me from behind and rammed his dick into my pussy with an unbelievable force. The penetration of his dick instantly made my pussy leak from pure wetness. The way in which he pounded his dick into my pussy and his balls hit against my clit caused an instant orgasm.

After a few more pounds with his dick, Monroe stopped, pulled out, and began to tongue fuck my ass. He used his finger and inserted it into my ass, causing my pussy to pulsate.

This went on for what seemed to be forever. I was at a total loss of words from this experience.

It was a different feeling, but one that I could get used to. I never expected to receive such pleasure from him in this manner. Bu, however he does it, I was sure enjoying it.

"I wanna fuck you in the ass, Monica. Instead of just taking it upon myself and doing it, I thought I'd get your answer on if it was okay or not."

"Tonight Monroe, you can do whatever it is you like. I have no complaints."

With the next thrust of his body, Monroe was pushing his dick inside my chocolate cave.

"Relax, baby. I got you, I will take it slow," Monroe instructed.

He then tried again, this time entering at a slower pace. My ass cheeks relaxed and he began to pump his dick in and out of my ass. The intensity of the pleasure caused me to orgasm numerous times back to back. I almost felt spent.

He pumped in and out a few more time and I could feel his dick throbbing inside of me. I knew exactly when he was going to bust and although I thought he had on a condom, He pulled his dick out and released his semen all over my ass and back.

"I'm not done with you yet, Monica. We still have some lovemaking to do."

Monroe grabbed another wash cloth and went into the bathroom to clean his dick off. When he returned, he still had an erection as big as day. I was turned on by this. I sat up, crawled on my knees to where he was standing, and took his dick into my mouth.

The taste of Irish Spring was still noticeable as I was sucking on it. Beginning at the head and slowing moving down the shaft, I attempted to take his entire dick into my mouth. Massaging his balls with my hands and sucking his dick with my mouth, I tried to give him just as much enjoyment as he was giving me.

Monroe began fucking me in my mouth with long deep strokes. He then intertwined his fingers in my hair to get a good grip and began moving my head back and forth. Just when I thought he was ready to release again he stopped and told me to get on my back and he would take it from there.

Monroe started eating my pussy once again, but just long enough to get the juices back flowing. He then climbed on top of me and began kissing me all over. With his knee, he spread my legs open so he could enter my paradise of love. He lifted my legs above my head, and in one slow swoop his dick had entered.

He slow grinded me to the rhythm of the music. He was so compassionate about everything he was doing, making sure I was pleased with the actions that were being performed.

He has rekindled the inner freak in me, and obviously, he had been keeping a little secret from me about the inner freak in him. I could get used to these lovemaking sessions if his desire and spontaneity was just as big as mine. My hunger for sex and the drive to please my partner was at an all-time high. Monroe had definitely done the job of making sure I was well taken care of

"There is more where that came from, Monica. If you allow us to let things happen naturally, it would be beneficial for the both of us. If you're open and willing to allow us to try new things, I believe we both will get the best out of this relationship," Monroe disclosed.

Monroe was right. I needed to loosen up and allow what's going to be...to be. Over the course of the next few months I had allowed the 'explorations' side of me loose and Monroe and I totally fell in love.

It was the best feeling ever and I'm glad my past didn't hinder me from finding someone to love me for who I am and not be judgmental towards the tangled web I had woven. Monroe doesn't know it yet, but I have a surprise for him also. I'm with child.

# FUCK ME

What you just say?

Fuck me is what I said.

Fuck me hard, fuck me slow,

Any way you want me.

I'mma do it

Fast or slow.

Fuck me! Dammit!!

Oh, I heard what you said,

I'm pounding in that pussy,

And you're kissing on my chest.

I'm guaranteed to give you my best.

How did you do it?

I rammed my dick inside of you,

And,

Your juices did the rest.

Showing evidence of what went on,

Between my dick and your vagina.

Fuck me harder.

Make me cum,

I want this nut to run.

Oh, I'm a skeeter didn't you know?

I have a tendency to really let it flow.

Oh, that's what you like?

You want to hear,

The sound my balls make,

 Against your clit?

You want to hear the sound I make,

As I pound deep inside that pussy?

Deep thrusting girl,

 Is what I give tonight.

Now that I have your

Fullest attention, it's my turn,

To be in charge.

My question to you is,

Can you take all this ten?

Ten inches is what I have,

Ten inches is what you get.

Of this strong, long hard stiff rock,

I'mma fuck you with.

Some call me king,

Some call me a ding.

Whichever one you please,

Just call it King ding a ling.

You wanna feel my cock,

As my dick stiffens like a rock?

Fucking that pussy with the king,

As it goes,

Keeta B.

In and out?

I'm gone fuck you right,

With this ten,

That's grown a lot.

Close your eyes, pretty lady,

And wait just a few more minutes.

I'mma give you what you been feigning.

Pardon me, it's not my intention,

To not pleasure you,

As you like.

I'm here to fulfill your wildest

Dreams and make 'em come

True tonight.

Eat me daddy.

Girl,

What did you say?

Eat me fast, eat me slow,

And tickle

My clit and make

Me show

You just what I like.

When you taste my juices

From my sweet nectar's

Delight.

Where Mami?

I wanna see it when it's,

Dribbling down your chin,

And you

Start all over again.

Eat me now.

Daddy,

Slow down just a little bit.

Baby, I wanna cum…

Wait,

But I still wanna have some fun.

Fuck it,

Take these juices in your mouth,

And don't you waste

One single drop.

I wanna give it all to you,

Just inside of me.

This is true.

Kiss me daddy.

Now,

Kiss me slow,

Put your tongue deep

In my mouth,

Tasting all of my sweet gum drops.

Swirl your tongue around,

Making sweet swooshing sounds.

Kiss me now.

Wait a minute, Stop!

I can't take it anymore.

My body's yearning for you,

To stick your dick

Inside of me.

So, let's do this to a tempo.

Suck me, Mami.

Suck on this juicy meat,

Then put it in your mouth.

Take it all in,

You know that's how we roll.

Use BOTH your hands to start,

Before you know it,

I'll be playing tonsil hockey

With your mouth.

My dick begins

Reaching to

The back of your mouth.

Suck the tip.

You heard me,

Deeper,

As I stimulate your clit.

Drop down,

Get on your knees,

As this ten goes deep within

In the wettest spot I know.

Slob all over it,

Like, you just can't get enough.

Fuck it, baby.

I can't wait.

Come here,

Bend over that couch,

And touch your toes.

Now listen very carefully,

I fucked you liked you told me.

So, tell me what you think.

Did I give you what you expected?

From getting all this dick?

Now, come on over here,

I'mma let you spend the night.

Keeta B.

So, close your eyes,

As I hold you tight.

And fuck you in your dreams.

# *PLAYER'S CLUB*

Who would have thought I'd be in the profession I'm in. My days consisted of long nights, short days with plenty of money to pay my bills. My clientele brought new meaning to the saying, "Make it Rain." The dollar bills were dropping and bottles were popping. This is the life of a local stripper day in and day out. It's dangerous in this type of profession, and the men can sometimes get a little too handsy. That's not one of my worries. My biggest fear would be to have one follow me home or find out where I lived, and I would have to kill him where he stood.

My stage name is Carmel Delight, but my real name is Kanisha Jones. I'm 21 years old, five-foot seven, brown skinned, and weigh approximately 125 pounds. I'm currently a student at Wayne County Community College in Detroit, Michigan, where I'm pursuing a degree in Marketing and Accounting. I have a 1-year-old son named Chris and strip at night to pay my tuition. Becoming a stripper wasn't what I planned to do with my life. Running with the wrong people, I kind of fell into this line of business by mistake. Growing up, I had dreams of attending a major university, pledging Delta Sigma Theta, and having a great career. However, things turned for the worst the last few months of my senior year in high school.

While most of my classmates were eagerly waiting for graduation and starting the next chapter in life, I was attending the funeral of my mother from a drug overdose. My mother and her live-in boyfriend had been doing drugs since I was in about the 3rd grade. Always trying to make my mother proud, I made sure to do my best in school and have the best grades I could possibly have. I wasn't a 4.0 student, but I was damn close, with a 3.965 GPA, and having accumulated scholarships from colleges and universities all around the nation. Many days we didn't have lights or food to eat, but I made sure all my studies were complete for the next day. Many of my close friends that I hung with knew what my home life was like, so they would bring me items to school to eat or save in my torn backpack to eat later. I was very appreciative of their acts of kindness.

When I was in about the 5th grade, my mom tricked me out for a dime bag and a shake. Two grown ass men had their way with me and I was on a downhill roller coaster ride from that day forward. One man unzipped his pants and shoved his erected dick into my young mouth. He pumped his hips back and forth until I felt as if though I had to throw up. I cried and cried, but there was no one to hear them. When he finished with me, he ripped off all my clothes and threw me down on the bed where he pinned me down by my arms, and with the same dick he had just shoved in my mouth, he was now ramming it into my virgin pussy. He covered my mouth to shield my cries. The feeling of humiliation was at an all-time high.

He started choking me with both hands as if that type of thing was normal. He finally got the nut he wanted and told me to get up off the bed and get cleaned up. Bleeding from my private area, I wobbled down the hall to the bathroom dizzy, in severe pain, and my pussy was swollen like a grapefruit. Thinking everything was over, another man barged into the bathroom and stated, "Hey pretty girl, the party is just starting. I hope you didn't think you were finished. Your mom owed us and she used you for the payment." Before I could say or do anything else, this man grabbed me and bent me over the bathtub and rammed his dick as far as he could into my ass. I cried and yelled for him to stop. It didn't do any good. He too choked me, slapped me, and then beat me until he came. He left me for dead in the bathroom. I vowed from that day forward I would do anything to get out of this situation and never turn back.

After this ordeal, I ran away several times and Child Protectives Services got involved. They mandated my mom to drug treatment and placed me in temporary foster care. My foster parents were the kind that didn't like kids. They only liked the checks that came with it. They would physically abuse the kids and misappropriate the funds. The husband was a sloppy drunk and pedophile. He liked to mess with the little boys that came into the home. Many nights, I would cry and try to devise a plan to run away again. I knew the system would only place me with another family. There was always the possibility the new family could be worse than the one I was currently with. I had no choice, given my circumstances. I had to leave before something happened to me.

After two weeks went by, I had devised a plan to run away. Taking only the clothes on my back and a few items to eat, leaving all else behind, I left in the middle of the night. It was awfully dark, raining, the winds were strong and high, and the temperature cold. I found myself sleeping on park benches, in gutters, under bridges, and on the steps of the library, with no one to call or come pick me up. Finally, I decided enough was enough. It was time I went to the group home run by the state foster care system. On my first day, one of the female care-givers trapped me in one of the counseling rooms and raped me. She told me how pretty I was and how she knew I would be a good treat. She slapped me around and punched me in my stomach repetitively before tearing off my skirt and ripping my panties. She tied my hands above my head and began to orally pleasure my pussy. She explained her art of cunnilingus and how she used her tongue to sexually stimulate not only herself, but me also. She stuck her fingers in my ass and pinched each of my breasts. It hurt like hell, but she obviously got something out of it. After about twenty minutes or so, she finally let me go. She put a knife up to my throat and said if I told anyone what happened she would kill me.

Scared and alone, I didn't tell a soul. This would be something I took to my grave. I felt torn by what had just transpired. I was an innocent young woman taken advantage of by someone who was supposed to be a role model.

Unaware of the proper names or acts of having sex I was at a total loss. Not knowing what to expect or if I should like what was happening I was scared out of my mind. Over the course of the last six months, my life has been turned upside down and inside out. I had been sexually violated, first by two men and now this woman. What the hell was happening to me? All of this because my mom chose to be a junky? Something had to give. I was tired of running away and no one would believe me if I told, so, I was forced to stick it out.

Over the next few months, the Department of Social Services along with Child Protectives Service conducted an undercover sting operation at the group home. Five care-givers and the administrators were taken into custody and fired from their positions for child endangerment, exploitation of minors, and having inappropriate relationships with children who were in the state's care. Finally, something was being done about the conditions and safety of those living in this home. I felt free, almost as if I had a chance at a new start. After the state's investigation, they closed down the home and sent all the kids from there to a bigger facility 20 miles away. This home was more updated and spacious. The staffing had a better ratio and each room accommodated four kids of the same sex, compared to the previous one that housed eight to ten per room.

By the time I turned fifteen, I had been in four group homes and with over 20 foster care families. But, throughout all of the back and forth and havoc that had torn my life to shreds, I still maintained the best grades in school. I not only was book smart, I was becoming street smart as well. Over time, I had developed perfectly. Nice, firm breasts, small waist, and an ass to die for. Group homes gave me the opportunity to meet all kinds of people from all walks of life. Each individual had their own experience to share. When I started to feel sorry for myself and all the things I had gone through, someone else told me their story and it would be twice as bad as mine. I decided to channel my inner anger and use it to be a positive force for someone else.

My mother had finally gotten well enough to kick her drug addiction. The state was allowing me to return to her care under semi-supervised conditions. They had given her keys to a new, completely furnished apartment, and four hundred dollars to buy clothes and food for the two of us. She was ordered to continue drug and family counseling and do a work program that taught her the necessary skills to find gainful employment. Things were starting to look up. My mom stayed clean for several months, well into the holiday season. For once, I actually had a decent Christmas where the gifts were wrapped and age appropriate. Finally, I felt safe and like we had a home.

Shortly after the holiday season, I began noticing little things started coming up missing from our apartment. It started with small appliances, radios, and watches. You know, the things a person wouldn't normally notice missing unless they had been around a crack head before. Once my laptop computer came up missing and I confronted my mother about it and she lied, I knew she had found her old habit once again.

First items came up missing, then we were getting shut off notices in the mail. Social Services issued my mother a check every two weeks and she got paid for going to those work enforcement classes. Why the hell was our shit getting cut off? Just when I thought things were stable, they once again became rocky. For six months we had a refrigerator full of food. I came home from school one day, opened the refrigerator door to make me a sandwich and all the damn food was gone. The only thing left was a carton of spoiled milk and some butter. I was fed up and something had to be done. I refused to be hungry or have to live in another foster care facility again.

One day, while sitting outside on the steps of my apartment, some of the older cats came up to me. I'd seen these dudes from around the way and they knew my mom and her situation. Big Dave was about 27 years old, dark skinned, 6'2", weighed every bit of 300 pounds and drove an old 87 Monte Carlo with a rag top. Big Dave liked to smoke weed and was known to trick the young girls out that lived in the neighborhood. I never paid him much attention and I prayed he'd do me the same.

This other dude named Mello was with him. Mello was 5'10", brown skinned, about 190, and only 20 years old. Mello was known as the weed man at my school. He had about five workers that I knew personally. Rumor had it he was recruiting young girls to become strippers. He would entice them with the hype of the money, and then he would get them drunk and high, drug them, and drop them off at the strip joint to dance. If the girls didn't do what he told them to, he would have one of his female friends beat the living daylights out of the girl.

Mello and I sat on the front steps of my apartment and talked after everyone else left. Music was bumping, the aroma of weed was high in the air, and I was grooving to the bass of each beat.

"You move really well. I love the way you move your body. You know how to sway your hips and allow your body to follow. Do you like dancing?" Mello asked.

"It must be my love for music. It's just something about the rhythm that makes my body move," I responded.

I noticed it had started getting dark. The wind blowing and the sound of the mosquitoes hitting the lamps brought a calm presence while sitting outside. It gave me a sense of peace. So much was happening in my life I just wanted to find peace. Mello inquired about how my mom was doing. He said he heard she was actually clean for a while.

I told him, "Yeah she was, but I think she's had a relapse."

"Why do you say that?" asked Mello.

"Because items are coming up missing from my house, there's no food to eat, and all of a sudden we getting shut-off notices. All the signs were present of her having relapsed just like before," I blurted out, full of emotions.

Mello looked at me with a sadness in his eyes, "I'm sorry, Nish, and I thought things were going good for you for a change. Is there anything I can do to help?"

Tears of anger and frustration instantly started flowing down my face. Never had I allowed the outside world to see me weak, my inner most fears or frustration, let alone see me cry. Before I could say or do anything, Mello put his arms around me and just held me. Kind of a reassurance that things would get better.

Before this day, Mello was never viewed as the compassionate type of guy. He was nice looking and known by everyone on the block, but I never thought he and I would have anything in common. He actually made me feel as if someone in the world cared about my well-being and what was happening to me. It gave me a sense of gratification.

It was getting late. Mello told me he would walk me to my door and make sure I got in safely. He was such a gentleman. We walked slow and continued talking. He held me close to him and I could smell the masculine scent of his cologne. Issey Miyake to be exact. The fragrance was intriguing and hypnotizing. He had a firm grip around my waist and it actually felt like I had somebody on my side.

As we approached my door, Mello stopped and pulled me to the side, then positioned me so I was facing him. He asked me if I minded going out to eat with him so we could talk some more. In shock and disbelief, I really didn't know what to say. Just when I was about to answer him, Mello stepped in front of me, pulled me in as close to him as humanly possible, then kissed me. He never allowed me to answer his question. I guess he already knew what my answer would be because he told me as I was walking into my apartment, "I'll see you in a couple days. I have some business to attend to, but I'll be by to pick you up for dinner, so be ready."

Unaware of what had just happened, my heart started racing fast. A boy, a D-boy (Dope boy) at that, was interested in me. Several days passed and just like he said he would, Mello called and told me to meet him outside the apartment around 5:45 p.m. Mello picked me up in Big Dave's car and drove me to the Golden Corral for a bite to eat. During dinner, we talked about life and things we both had going on. He asked about my grades and how school was going. In turn, I told him about my dreams of getting out of the projects and going to a major university. We both agreed that if I stayed focused and had a support team, then all things would be possible.

Mello and I started to hang out more often. Days turned into weeks and weeks turned into months. To prevent my lights from getting turned off, he started giving me money and stocked my refrigerator with food. My feelings for this guy were spinning out of control. I was really digging him. He was almost too good to be true, like a fairy tale, my knight in shining armor. He made me forget about the things that were troubling me. He took me out and showed me around to his friends. He even introduced me as his girlfriend to some of his relatives. I was truly and honestly flattered by his acknowledgement.

About two months or so after Mello and I started talking, we started having sex. Since we had spent lots of time together already he wasn't upset that I wasn't a virgin like most girls my age. Once I explained what happened, he actually felt sorry that those horrible things happened to me. He asked if he could introduce me to newer and exciting things. None of the things he mentioned or did to me compared to what happened when I was raped and forced to do the things those nasty bastards forced me to do. I felt love and compassion whenever Mello and I had sex. He took his time and pleasured me in more ways than one. The force and use of his tongue over my body was magical. His touch sent chills up and down my spine, causing instant eruption of sexual gratification. During many of our sexual encounters, Mello showed me the way he liked to be pleased. In the beginning, I felt as though it was demeaning and inhumane, but then I began to like it.

Mello would put a studded dog collar around my neck and tell me to get down on all fours. With his pants around his ankles he would have me walk over to him like a dog and suck him off. He got a rise out of pulling my hair and slapping me on my ass. The pain that shot through my body was so intense, but felt so good all at the same time. He liked to fuck me doggy style. He says it's because he could grip my ass and get a better angle at jabbing this pussy. How he would put it was: he was making sure I felt every inch of his dick up in me. Although it seemed like he was taking me too fast in the sex category, I was starting to love every minute of it. Over the course of several months, he began introducing females into our sexual encounters. The first few encounters, he allowed the females to just pleasure me, but then he wanted me to be a full participant. He wanted me to begin pleasing these women in the same manner they had done to me.

At first, I was nervous and didn't want to do it. He would constantly threaten to leave me high and dry if I didn't do what he said. This was a side of Mello I had never seen before but I didn't want to lose him. All emotional and caught up in my feelings for him, I knew eventually I would do it just for him. I reminded myself it's not like this was a regular occasion type thing. I started to believe I could get through it. Plus, I loved seeing the look on his face after we had sex. The look was priceless.

Mello loved to sit and watch the different females eat me out and perform sexual acts on me. He told me it turned him on and really aroused seeing that type of shit. He would sit in the corner watching, stroking his dick as different bitches took turns licking and sucking my clit and playing in my ass, causing me to have multiple orgasms. When it was my turn to return the favor he would get up out of his seat, pull his pants all the way down to his ankles, and mount me like a horse. He would slap my ass as hard as he could then turn around and fuck the shit out of me while I was eating the girl's pussy. The shit started to turn me on little by little.

By my senior year in high school, Mello and I had been messing around almost three years. He had turned me into a super freak at this point, and oh, how I'd grown to love this man and there was nothing in this world I wouldn't do for him. We'd had our share of ups and downs due to other bitches being jealous of what he and I had going on. I'd even gotten into some physical altercations over this man, but I was sticking with him through hell or high water. The sex was good and he was paying for me to keep my place. My mom was still getting high all the time so she was in and out, but at least I had a roof over my head. Mello was slowly turning me out and I didn't even see it.

Several more months rolled by, and things were looking up. Winter break was approaching and I would have a little time to rest up before my last semester of my senior year. College was still in my plans and I had prepared myself to take the different college entrance exams. Already knowing my mother's condition, continuous fight with drugs, and being in and out of rehab, going away to college would be out of the question. She needed me and even though she'd given me the sense of abandonment, I needed her also. Maybe if I could show her that by me going to college and getting a degree, I was going to make it better for the both of us, she would come around. Still having multiple opportunities to attend different colleges, I chose to attend a community college so I could stay close by and keep an eye out on her.

A few days before winter break, Mello came over to the apartment and wanted to chill. Normally we chilled at his crib or one of the spots he held down, but today was different. He said he didn't want to be around his partners or the hoes today. He just wanted it to be him and me. When he came over he seemed to be a little agitated. Where he would normally greet me with a smile, kiss on the lips, and bear hug me, he just walked right past me and into the apartment. When I asked if everything was okay, he only responded that he had a lot of things on his mind and just wanted to come chill to ease his mind. I was cool with that. I had tons of homework that needed to be done before the break started, and I wanted to share my news about where I had decided to attend school.

Instead of me sharing my news, Mello shared some with me. He told me he had been losing money on some of the girls that were working for him. Said he had to let a few of them go because they were too strung out on drugs and that life had gotten to them. Some of these were his best girls. Not only did they strip at the club during the week, they also hosted after party events for entertainment purposes. Mello told me that to help get his money back right he wanted me to start stripping on the weekends. Hesitant, nervous, scared, and new to all of this, I didn't know what to expect. I'd never taken my clothes off in front of anyone but him before. Even then, I was nervous and afraid. What the hell is this man doing to me? There was a knock on the door and Mello answered it. It was Big Dave.

"Man, is your girl down with getting this money or what?" Big Dave inquired.

Mello looked at Big Dave and replied, "I'm working on it, man. She is my girl and all. Give me a few minutes to finish talking to her and I'll be down in a sec."

Turning to me, Mello looked me in the eyes and spoke slowly. "Nish, look baby, I need for you to get out here and make this money. You know I wouldn't ask you if I thought it would be a bad idea. If you love me you'd do this for us. You'd be part of the Player's Club by doing this."

"Baby, you know what I've been through in life and I'm scared. What if something bad happens to me? Then what? Who is going to take care of me then?" I blurted out.

Mello responded, "You'll just have to trust me, babe."

Afraid of losing the one thing that seemed to matter to me at the moment, Mello, I started dancing at the Mystic Pyramid night club. Mello assured me it was only temporary until he got back the money that was stolen from Big Dave. I would be the main attraction for his come up. The club had me stripping on Friday's, Saturday's, and Sunday's. When I went on stage I was shaking and nervous before my first performance. Mello noticed how uptight I was so he brought me a drink to loosen me up. Once the liquor was in my system the moves and gyrations came easily. On one particular night, I made over five hundred dollars from lap dances and another seven hundred from my stage performances. The audience liked me so much they named me Carmel Delight. Mello expressed to me how well I did for my first night and that it would only get better.

After my shift had ended, Mello took me home that night. We drank, got high, laughed at one another, and enjoyed the remainder of the evening. Inside my apartment, he had the music playing sultry soul jazz and the candles were lit. He had run me some bath water, and had candles all around the tub. Mello undressed me, slowly admiring every inch of my body. I eased my aching body into the tub and Mello washed and caressed every inch of it. Mello rubbed my feet, my legs, arms, and neck. When he wasn't rubbing and touching me, he slowly placed succulent kisses all over me. He stood me up and pat dried my entire body, then guided me into my bedroom where he lay me down and sexed me up, causing me to moan, groan, and beg for more. When we finished we just held one another and fell asleep in each other's arms.

The next day, Mello woke up and told me he needed to make a run. Before he left, he asked me how I enjoyed being a part of the Player's Club. Turning to him I asked, "What all does being in this club consist of?"

"It entails you making this money by shaking your ass on stage in front of a few niggas. Every now and again, you do a couple private parties where you get butt ass naked and perform a few sex acts. Lastly, you as my girl, get top priority amongst the other bitches I fuck with in this game."

Did I just hear the man whom I love with every inch of my body just blatantly admit that he fucks with other bitches? What kind of shit is that? Here I am thinking it's me and him in this thing together and he out here with other hoes.

"I will have to really think things over, Mello. It's a lot of stuff you just threw at me and I need time to digest everything," I responded.

Mello looked at me in disgust. "Bitch, you bet not take all day with an answer. We got this money out here to be made and I told you, I need you to assist me in getting it. Either you down or you ain't. Either way, it's going to be gotten."

I started to feel as if he was pressuring me to dance and shit. The dancing wasn't what bothered me, it was the taking off my clothes that did. How could a man want and insist his woman take off her clothes in the presence of total strangers? This can't be the type of love I been trapped in for the last several months.

This Player's Club shit didn't seem all it was cracked up to be and I didn't want to have any parts of it. I got up the nerves to tell Mello that he and his boys were going to have to find another way of getting that bread. I knew he could become violent and not take the news well. I prepared myself for the worst.

After I had given Mello the spill about me not wanting to shake my ass for a living, he brutally beat and raped me. He had several of his homeboys sodomize me with unknown objects and kick and punch me. He then had the nerves to kiss me in my mouth when he was finished. My eye were swollen shut but I knew his touch and the sound of his voice. This would be a day I would never forget.

The love I once knew was no longer. I was hurt in more ways than one. The person who I thought and believed would understand why I wouldn't want to subject my body to the subjects of others was the one person who hurt me the most. My biggest fear was always that one of the clients would get too possessive and follow me home and do something terrible to me, but instead it was the guy I trusted with my entire being. Never in life would I forget the rules of the Player's Club.

Approximately three years had passed. I had finally regrouped and finished my degree at Wayne County Community College. Things were looking up for me. During my last semester of school, I had the opportunity to do an internship with a great company, Curcuru & Associates, CPA. At the end of my term they offered me a permanent, full-time position.

It was everything I needed. The position offered great benefits, school reimbursement, bonuses, and the ability for advancement within the company. I knew with hard work and dedication this could lead into a career position. The people I worked with were awesome. They made sure I learned everything possible and then some. The best part of this was the job was so busy, it took my mind off all the bad and negative things that had happened to me over the course of the years. It molded me into a better person. My mom's death still had me emotional from time to time, but I didn't allow it to consume me. I knew if she was alive she would be proud of me.

Just when I had given up hope of finding love or affection from a man, this attractive looking guy who worked for another firm contacted me. He asked me out on a lunch date for simple conversation and a cup of coffee. After everything that had happened to me, I was a tad bit nervous about seeing this man. Sometimes I felt the more I tried to hide my past the more it crept up on me. It was pure foolishness, but I couldn't fight the feeling. After praying about it and speaking with my therapist, I decided to give it a try.

Chad was a wonderful guy. He was polite, attentive, and well mannered. It was the simple things he did that impressed me. He pulled out my chair before I sat, offered me his jacket when he noticed I was cold, and he always gave me direct eye contact when I spoke, to reinforce the fact that he was giving me his undivided attention. He was a true gentleman. He made me realize the treatment I received before was not that of a man but a boy. He showed me how to have an intellectual conversation that had substance and meaning. Chad treated me like a lady, and I needed that.

Chad and I began dating over the course of the next six

months. My feelings for this man were growing more intense. He showered me with luxurious gifts, wined and dined me, and took me to cultural museums. He stimulated my mind, body, and soul, making me feel warm inside. Something I had never felt before. We began sharing personal details about our past. During one of our conversations, I shared with him my relationship with Mello and the Player's Club, how my mom was a drug addict who sold me for a fix to two men who raped me. I also shared my encounter with the foster care system and how they allowed one of their employees to sexually assault me as well. By the time I finished sharing the details of my past, tears were streaming down my face. Chad took a piece of tissue and wiped my tears away.

Now it was Chad who indulged in the sharing. He shared with me how when he was a teenager his home was broken into and he watched as the burglars killed his parents in front of him. He then told me how he was sent to live with his aunt who didn't have any children, but she only took him in to reap the benefits of the check that came along. As he went down memory lane, I could see the pain in his eyes. He finally blurted out full of emotions, "If it hadn't been for my grandmother and the love she had for me, I don't know where I would be today." I knew the pain he was feeling. For I, too, had been down that long road. With our emotions on high, I wrapped my arms around Chad to console him and let him know he was not alone.

That night, we began to kiss uncontrollably, then unexpectedly, we made love. It was nothing like my past experiences. What I thought was love with Mello was far from it. What I was experiencing with Chad at this very moment sent electrifying impulses throughout my entire body. A warm feeling came over me. Could this be the love I'd been seeking my entire life?

During the lovemaking session that I experienced with Chad, he took his time with me. He kissed and tasted every inch of my body. The warm, masculine touch of his hands over my entire body sent chills up and down my spine. The gentle touch of his wet, succulent lips as they brushed against my skin caused vibrations to pulsate throughout my vagina. The oral pleasure he gave caused my body to twinge and convulse repeatedly. This was a real man showing a woman what it was like to be loved. Not wanting him to think I was too good to return the favor, when he finished exploring every inch of my body, I took his manhood into my mouth and teased it with my tongue. Gentle strokes of my hand on his erect dick gave Chad added pleasure. I wanted him to feel just as wanted as he had made me feel and then some.

Just when I thought the life before me had taken every ounce of me away. Chad stepped in and showed me that no matter what life has thrown in your path, you must pick up the pieces and glue them back together then press on. Two years from the date Chad and I started dating, we were married. Good bye old life, hello new.

# *WHAT DOES IT TAKE*

What would it take to get you hot?
Does your pussy get instantly wet
As the beat drops?

I wanna know what really turns you on.
Is it the girth in my pants, or the
thickness of my   tongue?

Is it the size of my feet, or the tricks my fingers do?
When they enter your creamy tunnel
Tucked secretly between your thighs of thunder?

Touch me, tease me, anyway you
Wanna please me.

I'm down for this moment of sexual EXCITEMENT.
Let me kiss you all over,

And caress your body like no other
Could

Possibly do to you in the manner
I would.

I want you to climb on top of me.
Take control of my body.

Keeta B.

Tantalize my mouth with your tongue.
 Let me feel the warmth

From your wet nature on my dick before I cum.
Let me flip you over and put this dick on your ass.

Let me smack your left cheek
And make the right one mad.

As my lips trace every inch of your back,
And my hand reaches around

And grabs your nice firm breasts.
Caressing and squeezing is what I do best.

My dick is getting harder
And your pussy is getting warmer.

I can't resist feeling inside of you
And receiving the ultimate thunder.
Let me make your juices explode.
All while swimming
In your natural wet whirlpool of blunder.

Kiss me on my neck.
Now touch my rock-hard chest.
Do you like what you feel?

If you haven't noticed,
I'm trying to impress you
With my sex appeal.

Let's play a game
Of hide and seek.

My dick deep inside your pussy
Searching for your wetness
Do you see my nature rising?

To greet you like we've never met?
Kiss on him.
Talk into the mic.

The studio's all yours
Do what ya like.
Tell him how you really feel.

How you wanna hold him tight.
Go ahead,
Suck on the tip.

Make my body come to life.
Get the juices in your mouth
Flowing.

Now spit just a little bit and suck it right back up.
Pleasuring me with your mouth
And I will lick you with this tongue.

Keeta B.

Show me what you're working with
And I'll show you how it's done.
Pretend you're sucking
On your favorite flavor popsicle.

I wanna hear you slurp.
I promise to return the favor,

When my tongue tastes your sweet,
Ripe Georgia peach,
And have all the juices flowing.

We're gonna mess up some sheets tonight
From all the passion that will fill the air.
You'll be saying "I Love You."

Before, the night is through.
Don't touch that switch!
Leave it alone.

We don't need a ceiling fan,
 Let me hear you moan.
 I want to feel the sweat drip
From our bodies,

As if we were stranded on a deserted island.
Forget 69.

I got a new position I wanna try.
360 is my new style of fucking

So let's stop talking and start working.
I plan on spinning you around

In a 90-degree angle, all while my dick is inside
Of your pussy while we're fucking.

Then I'm gonna spin myself around
Another 90 degrees
So that our asses touch each other

And I'm fucking you with ease.
Can you feel the intensity of me?

As I fuck you in and out?
Good, I would hate to disappoint you,

Even on the first try.
Still, we have another 180 degrees to go.

How would you like it fast or slow?
So, am I making you hot?

Have I reached the point of climax?
Where you cum on command?

Have I touched every inch of you yet?
If not, let me continue,
I want you wet.
Me on top of you with your legs bent back.

You on top, me straddled to the back.
You on your back with your legs
Behind your head,
While I'm in a chair position

Pounding this pussy
With all my might.

Get on your knees, let's do this again.
One of us better bust a nut soon
Or we'll both be spent.

Oh yass, the juices are flowing now,
I can feel them on my dick
A few more pounds
And I'm gonna release these kids.
Now I ask you one more time,
What did it take?

THE ART OF FRUITING
Ladies, have you ever heard of the technique
Called Grape Fruiting your man?

The sexual act of using fruit
To satisfy and pleasure your man.
Giving him the tantalizing feeling
He won't be able to resist?

The feeling of getting head
And pussy at the same time?

Oooo shit it makes his dick
Rock hard just thinking 'bout it.
How, you say?

By following
A few simple instructions
And you'll be on your way.

First get the fruit,
Slice it in half
Be sure you make a hole
By carving out the center
Now place it firmly on his shaft
Making sure his dick will fit.

Put the ring on one side
Sliding it on down over the head
Now place your mouth on it
Beginning at the tip.

Start sucking nice and gentle
You want to get him
To the point
Where he wants to explode.

Now,
Take the test,
Show off your skills
It's not very hard
You know what to do.

Keeta B.

The sexual act
Of pleasuring your man.
Pleasure him orally
Without using your hands.

Make it fun for him by
Only using your mouth
You know that is the hole
That gets sloppiest.

He's ready, about to bust a nut,
From the thought of you
Sucking him up.

Visualizing you
As your mouth drools his nut.
Make your man cum
All over your face.

Show him you're down.
Soon it will be his turn
To return the favor.

Do you remember?

When you were young,
You would tell the boys
How you wanted them
To kiss your fruit cocktail.

Then, as you got older
You soon realized
Exactly what you were saying?

It was nasty back then
How were asking for oral pleasure.

Any man would love
To lick
Your fruit full of passion.

Damn, you're making me horny.
It's time to explore
Get in touch with your exotic side
Allow your inner beast to roar.

Sex up your mate and make them feel complete
Give them all you got
Shout it

To the mountain top
Let him be your Tarzan while
You be his Jane

Swing from his vine and let him taste
Of your grapes
The sounds of lovemaking
Should sound through the jungle
All the wild animals begin to wonder.

How the art of fruiting wasn't
Already a contender.
A solidified requirement by those
Who don't have to wonder?

What it's like to be
A freak in the bed
Juices overflowing,
Fantasize with your partner
Even role play.

Pretend to be a stripper
Sliding up and down his pole,
Or a Macarena dancer with a fruit bowl.

Whichever one you choose
Make sure you follow through
By enticing your mate
With your art of fruiting.

# CRAVINGS

I was sitting alone in the office when the thought of him crossed my mind. Immediately my legs shifted and crossed themselves. I was thinking about how great he felt when he was inside me. As my pulse began to make a home in my pussy, the throbbing became so intense that I let out a silent moan in hopes that no one walked in and heard me. Damn, I wanted him. I began to look around as I slowly placed my right hand between my legs and pressed hard, massaging while my left hand gripped my breasts. Hmm, no one noticed. I decided this might be the perfect time to take a bathroom break...so to the stall I went with my phone in my hand. I quickly dialed his number, not knowing if he would answer since he was working as well. But to my surprise, he did.

I didn't greet him like I normally do. The only thing that came out of my mouth was, "I want you and right now I am alone touching myself, imagining that you were inside me."

Wow, I must have caught him off guard because all he could say was, "Really now?"

So I continued on to tell him how my black lace boy shorts has become wet from my moisture and how they were no longer a part of my wardrobe. How my shirt revealed the hardness of my erect nipples that longed to be caressed by his tongue. How my mouth was begging to be coated by his warm cum...and how I had three fingers deep in me as we were speaking. "Just so you know, when you come home, I will be waiting at your front door with a soaking wet pussy and a warm moist mouth, both desiring to be filled with your dick! So please don't make me wait!"

His silence was exactly what I expected as I continued to fuck myself as I stood in the stall with one leg perched on the seat. Suddenly, I heard him say, "Cum for me, baby!" And just like that, my body responded with a massive eruption. My legs and shoes were now soaked from the explosion that he commanded from me. I moaned, "I came for you, daddy. Just like you told me."

And he simply replied, "Good girl, I'll see you later."

Now, when I arrived at his home after work, to my surprise, he was already there. Before I could get out of my seat belt, the front door opened, but he was nowhere in sight. As I walked in, he came from behind the door, put his hand around my neck and said, "Get on your knees!" I almost came immediately as I lowered myself to the floor knowing exactly what he wanted from me. He dropped the towel from his freshly showered body and grabbed my head, pushing his dick towards me. I opened my mouth and took him all in. My mouth began to water at the first taste. Damn, now this is what I've been craving all day. My tongue began to make circles and figure eights around his veiny manhood as he held my head in place and dared me to take him past my gagging point. I wanted this, I needed this. Hell my pussy wanted this and damn sure needed this. My pussy was definitely responding to this! After a few minutes, he pulled me up by my hair and commanded that I undress. And you already know I did.

Once I was naked, he picked me up, sat me on his dick, pushed my back against the wall, and fucked me caveman style! I felt like I was suspended in mid-air, helpless as he fucked me with deep, hard strokes. He walked me over to the sofa and told me to lie back as he held my legs on his shoulders and fucked me like I've never been fucked before. You would've swore we were auditioning for our own movie. He was my personal porn star and I was his. I came so hard that I damn near cried, but I swear they would've been tears of pure pleasure and joy. My body became limp from the torture that he was putting it through, but I'd be lying if I said I wasn't enjoying every minute of it!

He was nowhere near done with me, so he flipped me over and wrapped his arm around my neck and entered me slow so that I could feel every inch of his dick as it filled my pussy. I moaned and began to cum uncontrollably. He loved that shit so he began to fuck me slowly and passionately, as he used his forearm to choke me firmly. I was his sex slave and he was my master. My body was his for the taking. My legs were shaking uncontrollably, so he bent me over the ottoman and pulled my ass up to the perfect spot for him to finish me off. I was drained, but I was enjoying his dick so much that I wasn't going to quit. He put his hands around my waist and pulled me back on his dick as he continued to fuck me senseless. When I tried to take a break, he'd scratched my back and told me, "Grind on this dick like you want it!" And, of course, you know I did.

When it came time for him to cum he grabbed my hair, pulled my head around, and came in my face. I was so fucking turned on that all I wanted was to have him inside of me again, so I did what I thought was best and put him in my mouth and began to suck his dick, taking every drop of cum that he had left. This man tasted so damn good to me that I had to have him inside of me again, but my body was weak and so was he, so we retired to the bed, but not before promising each other that before the night's end there would be a round two and three!

Written by Guest Writer Keybae

# *ABOUT KEETA B.*

Keeta B. is a well-established author with three books under her belt, which includes: *Life's Memories*, *Unforeseen Partitions* and part 2 of the same. She is recognized for her erotic based lit, as well as heart capturing true stories about her own life. Keeta B. hopes to keep her readers globally interest at the highest peak as their minds remains curious as to what she has in store next.